SAVAGE *release*

Savage Angels MC Series Book Ten

Kathleen Kelly

Savage Release

Savage Angels MC Series Book Ten

Kathleen Kelly

All efforts have been made to ensure the correct grammar and punctuation in the book. If you do find any errors, please e-mail Kathleen Kelly: kathleenkellyauthor@gmail.com

Thank you.

Disclaimer: The material in this book contains graphic language and sexual content and is intended for mature audiences, ages 18 and older.

ISBN: 978-1-922883-07-0

Re-editing by Swish Design & Editing
Proofreading by Swish Design & Editing
Book design by Swish Design & Editing
Cover design by Clarise Tan at CT Cover Creations
Cover Image Copyright
First Edition 2018
Second Edition 2021

DEDICATION

For everyone who's been on this journey with me.
It's been a wild, fun ride.

Thank you for loving the Savage Angels MC as much as I do.
The boys are near and dear to my heart, and I'm so happy you purchased this book.

Enjoy book ten :)

SAVAGE
release

CHAPTER 1

RENNY

Burns, the prison guard, is eyeballing me as I stand behind the last gate on my way out of this hellhole. If I were still a guest of the state, I'd be looking at the concrete, but this fucker can't hurt me anymore. Glenford Maximum Security Prison has been my home for eight fucking years.

But Destiny finally did it.

My kid sister said she'd get me out, and she did.

"See you soon, Bennett." Burns smirks as he walks away without a backward glance.

"Not fucking likely," I murmur.

Being in Glenford, there isn't a lot to do except exercise. The clothes I came into this place with are in a brown paper bag. Destiny brought me some jeans, a black T-shirt, and boots. At least they fit.

The gate buzzes, and I stride out of this place, which has taken so much from me. Once I am outside with those gates behind me, I close my eyes and inhale.

Fresh, *free* air.

Nothing has tasted sweeter.

"Renny?"

My head snaps toward the voice—Destiny. She's become a head turner—long dark hair, a figure any woman would be proud of, and the face of a damn angel.

Tears stream down her cheeks as she throws her arms around my neck. I engulf her in a hug, lift her off her feet, and swing while she laughs and squeals.

"Hey, sis, it's good to be free."

I let her go, but Destiny moves her hands to my shoulders and leans back, a smile on her pretty face. "I've missed you." She wipes under her eyes.

"Right back at you."

"Clothes, okay?"

I step back from her and hold my arms out. "Yeah. They fit good." I glance over my shoulder at the gate. "Can we get the fuck out of here?"

Destiny belts out a laugh. "Fuck, yes." She puts her hand in mine and pulls me toward a black Escalade. A man is standing there, hair falling over half his face, one blue eye tracking our movements. Instinctively, I put Destiny behind me.

The fucker chuckles and holds out his hand. "I'm

Kade Cantrill, Destiny's fiancé."

Destiny shuffles around me and latches onto his other arm. "Renny, I told you about Kade."

Gripping his hand hard, I shake it and grunt out the words, "Yeah, yeah, you did."

He's a big fucker, but I'm taller. I'm six foot seven, and after spending eight years with nothing to do but build muscle, I'm a mountain compared to him. Releasing his hand, I step back and smile.

"You want to drive?" Kade asks me.

"Nah, no license. Last thing I need is the cops pulling us over and busting me for some bullshit infraction."

Kade nods and opens the passenger back door. I move to get in the car, but Destiny squeezes my bicep and hops in the car.

"Nope, you're up front. I'm in the back."

"I'm good in the back."

"Renny, I'm a good foot shorter than you. You need all the leg room you can get. Get in the front."

"Only a foot?" I tease.

Destiny laughs as I walk around the car and climb in.

"Nice wheels."

Kade looks at me. "Not mine. It belongs to Dane. He's the president of the Savage Angels MC in Tourmaline."

"I know who he is."

He starts the car, and I hit the button to roll down

the window. "A few of your kind were in Glenford."

"My kind?" Kade tilts his head to the side, a scowl on his face.

"Yeah, MC members."

He huffs, and the scowl disappears. "Right."

Destiny's hand lands on my shoulder. "Kade and I bought an old house."

"That's an understatement." Kade grins. "It was barely standing."

Destiny laughs and hits his arm. "It was not *that* bad."

"You're right, it was worse," Kade counters.

Destiny shakes her head and says, "We've almost finished the renovations. Your room is all done up. It's one of the best in the house."

"I'm staying with you?"

Destiny nods. "Of course, you're family."

Staring at Kade, I ask, "Are you okay with that?"

He shrugs a shoulder up on one side. "Is there a reason I wouldn't be? Family takes care of family."

My baby sister has him wrapped around her little finger. I smile at her, then stare out the open window at the view. The fresh air on my face feels like heaven, and I close my eyes, but only for a moment, to enjoy the feel of it. After being away for so long, I don't want to miss a thing.

Destiny is prattling away in the back seat, and I nod or grunt a yes or no to her many questions.

Do I like broccoli?

Do I like carrots?

Do I like meatloaf?

Her questions feel endless.

For eight years, I was told when to eat, sleep, and shit. *Do I like broccoli?* Fuck if I know. Whatever was put in front of me, I ate. The only thing I really liked was at Christmas when the warden would let us have apple pie and ice cream. This I coveted and would stab any motherfucker who would try to steal it.

"Renny?"

Twisting in my seat, I stare at Destiny. "Yeah?"

"Do you like Italian?"

"I used to like pizza."

Destiny agrees with a slight incline of her head. "I thought we'd go somewhere nice for your first night out, but we can do pizza."

"I'm happy to do whatever you want."

"Tonight, we're staying in a hotel, and tomorrow we'll fly home."

"Home?"

"Tourmaline," replies Kade.

"What about the car?"

"Dane is going to drive it back. He's been with Kat, promoting her new album. He's bringing her home."

"The Grinders' chick?"

"Yeah, she's his ol' lady. She's also pregnant."

"Right, saw that on the news."

Destiny smiles. “Kat has been on a rampage lately. I think her back is killing her.”

“Yeah, well, twins will do that,” replies Kade.

“She’s having twins?”

Destiny nods. “Yeah, it runs in Dane’s family. This is her second set. Kat’s not very far along, but she already looks like she’s six months pregnant. Judging by her previous pregnancy pictures, it seems she’s going to be larger this time around.”

“At least.” Kade chuckles.

Destiny swats at his arm again and directs her gaze toward me with her big brown eyes. “I’m so glad you’re coming home. Rush wanted to be here to see you out of that horrible place, but he had clients.”

Devon ‘Rush’ Rushard is Destiny’s boss and mentor. He took Destiny under his wing after she graduated from law school, and without him, I’d still be in prison. I owe him and Destiny a debt I can never repay.

“I’ll meet him soon enough.”

“Yep, at the party.”

“Kade!”

“What party?”

Destiny shakes her head at Kade. “It was supposed to be a surprise. It’s a little get-together so you can meet some of our friends.”

Facing straight ahead, my lips turn down, and I sigh. “I’m not big on huge gatherings with people I don't know."

Destiny giggles. "It's why we're having a party, so you can get to know them."

"Sis, I'm not sure I'll—"

"It's all arranged. Everyone's excited to meet my big brother."

"There's a gas station ahead. I need a Pepsi, and we can fill it up too. Babe, would you mind going in, paying, and getting drinks and snacks?"

"Of course. Renny, what would you like?"

Having been away for so long, I've got no idea. "I'll have what Kade is having."

"Pepsi?"

"Yeah."

Kade pulls in beside a pump, and Destiny opens her door. "You sure you don't want a Coke?"

"Whatever is easier."

She smiles at me. "You used to drink Coke. I'm getting you a Coke."

I give her a chin lift, and Kade waits until she's inside the gas station before he opens his door. "Get out and stretch your legs. We've got another two hours before we hit the hotel."

Sliding out of the car, I move around to stand near Kade. His eyes are fixed on the gas station.

"She means well. Destiny fought for you for so long. Getting you out was all she could think about. Trust me when I tell you the people she wants you to meet want nothing from you but to meet you.

Everyone knows you've been through a lot. We all know Glenford isn't a cakewalk. Destiny doesn't have a huge number of friends. It's been study and work. I know it's not fair on you, but if you could give her this, it'd mean the world to her."

Kade Cantrill is smart. He knows after being cooped up for so long, I'm not exactly social. The idea of spending time with a bunch of strangers in a new town isn't what I want. I wanted to check the place out, slowly get to know those around me, and decide if it was safe.

"I owe her. I'll do it."

Kade shakes his head. "You don't owe her. Destiny loves you. She never believed for a minute you were guilty. When she loves someone, she's all in."

"Is that why you're letting me stay with you? To keep her happy?"

Kade grins. "Partly, but I meant it when I said you're family." He puts the pump away and replaces the cap on the gas tank. "I'm worried about her. You've been her soul focus for a long time. Everything she did was to get you out, and now that you are, I'm worried where her focus will fall."

"The wedding." I stretch my arms above my head, and Kade squints at me. "I'll do this party, but man, when it's done, I'm going to point her to wedding shit. Be prepared for her new focus to be on you."

Kade appears somewhat relieved. "She's been working her whole life for this moment. You're right. The wedding will help, but then what do I do?"

"Kids."

Kade's eyes go wide. "Whoa! We haven't even had that conversation. Hell, I'm not sure I'm dad material."

Chuckling, I walk around the Escalade and get back in. The idea of becoming an uncle warms my heart. I never thought I would see my sister pregnant and growing a child. Hell, getting out of prison is something I never thought would happen.

Thea.

Her name whispers across my mind, and the warm feeling in my chest turns to ice.

Did I ever love her the way Kade loves Destiny?

Did she ever love me the way Destiny loves Kade?

Even as I ask myself these questions, I know the answer is no.

If Thea did, she would never have turned on me. Finding and punishing her and those who put me in Glenford have kept me alive. My one burning ambition while inside was to either live long enough to do my entire bid in prison or get out and end them. Either way, I am going to track them down like the scum they are and put them in the ground.

Destiny doesn't know it, but I'm not the same

man. They put me away for a triple murder, but I didn't do it. Now I have a list of those who betrayed me and more than three people on it.

Thea North
Jackson MacKenzie
Steve Plant
Hunter Johns
Samuel Perth
Derrick Long

These names are seared into my brain, and I repeat them to myself every night like a mantra. They *will* all pay for what they took from me. My face will be the very last thing they see as they inhale their final breath.

The hotel room is nice, certainly better than I'm used to.

Destiny reserved me a single room while she and Kade are in the room next door.

I needed a moment of peace to exist without what felt like an endless stream of questions. Kade gets it and tries to curb Destiny's curiosity about all things me, but she keeps on asking.

A knock sounds on my door, and I groan as I approach. On the other side is Dane Reynolds. He's as big as he seems on the television.

Thrusting out his hand, he says two words, "Dane Reynolds."

We shake.

"Renny Bennett."

Dane grins, exposing perfectly straight white teeth. "Good to finally meet you. I'm headed down to the bar for a drink. Want to join me?"

"Sure."

I follow the behemoth to the elevators. His hair is tied back in a man bun, and he's dressed almost the same as me, except he's wearing his cut.

The doors open, and a little old lady is inside. Her eyes go wide at the sight of the two of us. Dane stands near her, but I try to keep as far away as possible.

"Hey, nice day outside, isn't it?" Dane asks the woman.

She clutches her handbag to her chest. "Yes," she replies curtly. She doesn't look at him, but he doesn't seem to care that we scare her.

"Have you tried the restaurant downstairs?"

She glances up at him. "What? No."

"Best steak I've had in a good long while. My wife likes the chicken."

The woman says nothing, only nods, and as soon

as the doors open, she steps out and hurries away.

Dane chuckles. "I tried."

"Why even try?"

Dane's eyebrows shoot up to his hairline. "To make her feel comfortable. We don't exactly appear friendly, especially you with your prison tats on your neck."

"Yes, I may have gotten them in prison, but a professional tattoo artist did them."

Dane's lips turn down. "It's all about being better."

My sister's friends are checking me out. I'm sure he read my file. I'd bet money he had his men look into my background before I got out of Glenford. And now he's trying to make a none-too-subtle point.

"I'm not the man I was before I went away."

Dane sits at the bar and signals for the bartender, who meanders our way.

"Whiskey, no ice."

The bartender makes eye contact with me.

"Coke."

The bartender puts our drinks in front of us and moves farther away.

"Coke?"

"I want my first drink to be with Destiny. She deserves a few of my firsts."

He sips his drink and grits his teeth as he swallows.

"What do you want to know?"

Dane pivots on the seat, glass in hand, and gives me the once-over. "Are you going to bring trouble to my house?"

Confused, I shake my head. "I'm not staying with you. I'm staying at Destiny's place."

Dane taps the bar top. "Tourmaline *is* my house. You might not have done what they imprisoned you for, but you were into some bad shit."

"I didn't do it."

"Good. I like Destiny… she's good for Kade. Kade and Zeke are good for the club. They have a calming influence, and, brother, I like peace."

His piercing blue eyes and steel voice wash over me. Dane Reynolds is letting me know I can't fuck up his home, not that I'm going to.

"I'm not here to make trouble for you or anyone Destiny is close to. Yes, I have unfinished business, but I'll make sure it doesn't blow back on you or my sister."

Dane takes another sip of his drink, but it goes down easier this time. "Eight years is a long time to plot revenge." He puts his glass down. "Make sure you think it through. You can have a good life in Tourmaline. The people are good." He chuckles. "Even the law is easy to get along with so long as we don't piss Carlos off."

"Carlos?"

"Town sheriff. Most days, we like each other."

"I won't be any trouble to your club. When I seek out my enemies, they won't see me coming."

"A few of mine are in Glenford. Did you know Boxer?"

"Scrawny fucker with a scar running up his left arm?" Dane nods. "Yeah, sold him cigarettes and candy bars occasionally."

"Boxer says you're okay."

"He's doing it tough with some of the new inmates."

Dane frowns. "Yeah, we figured. Boxer isn't one to complain, but the last time his ol' lady visited him, she said he was jumpy as fuck."

"The White Power Brotherhood is making life difficult for him."

"Fucking white supremacist assholes."

It's nice to know my sister's friends aren't racist douchebags.

"Boxer can take care of himself. He's tough."

Dane nods. "Yeah. He got screwed going to Glenford. The judge made an example out of him. He should have gone somewhere a little closer to home."

"They're trying to keep the gangs separated."

"Except it doesn't work, does it?"

"Nah, they all find new gangs once they're inside. It's better to be with a gang than on your own."

Dane picks up his glass and swallows the rest of the amber liquid. "You didn't."

With a smile, I take a sip of my Coke. “Nope. I like my company just fine.”

“You ever think about joining up?”

“You asking me if I’m interested in the Savage Angels?”

Dane tilts his head from side to side. “Maybe.”

“I’m not opposed to it.”

“You’d have to start from the bottom up.”

“I don’t mind being a prospect. Right now, all I want is to find my place again. Get a home, a job, and keep to myself.”

“And your revenge?”

“Will come in its own good time.”

Dane swivels back around and holds his empty glass up to the bartender. “We’re always hiring mechanics.”

“You offering me a job?”

“Maybe. When you’re settled in at Tourmaline, come to the clubhouse. If the guys like you, we’ll see.”

“Destiny has arranged a party.”

Dane smiles. “I know.”

“Are any of your kind going to be there?”

“Yep. Just about all of us.”

“*Great.*”

Dane belts out a loud laugh. “You’ll be fine. Destiny talked you up. Everyone is excited to meet you.”

“You’re not helping.”

"Make an appearance. Stay an hour, two tops, then sneak away. Destiny might want to show you off to everyone, but many of us know what it's like to be cooped up and then set free. You've been institutionalized for eight years, and that doesn't go away overnight. The guys will understand even if your sister doesn't."

He gets it. It's not the party but the break-in routine. Hell, even sitting at this bar is strange. It's nearly seven o'clock. For eight years, I ate at five, we had an hour for socialization, and then back to our cell. I'm starving.

Destiny walks into the bar, and half a dozen heads turn in her direction. She doesn't notice as she makes a beeline for me.

"Here you are! I've been knocking on your door." Destiny rests a hand on Dane's arm. "Kat found me, and she said you'd be here. She needs ice cream."

Dane sighs. "Did she say what flavor?"

"You don't know?"

He scrubs a hand over his face. "Last week it was chocolate, but then she changed it to cookie dough over the weekend. So, no, I have no fucking clue."

"Salted caramel."

Dane stands. "You sure?"

"Yep." Destiny giggles.

Dane holds out his hand to me, and we shake. "I'll see you in Tourmaline. Good meeting you, Renny."

"When I'm settled, I'll come see you about that job."

Dane gives me a chin lift. "Sounds good." He strides out of the room.

Destiny scooches up onto Dane's seat, a frown between her brows. "You're already getting a job?"

"Maybe. They want to give me a once-over."

"I thought you'd want to settle in first. Get the lay of the land, so to speak."

"Routine is good for the soul. Besides, I need to pay you and Rush back."

"Renny, you don't owe me anything."

"Destiny, I've got four hundred dollars in my bank account. I'm pretty sure this hotel is more than that, and you spent a lot of hours working to get me out. All of it costs money. I need to pay you back."

She reaches out and puts her hands around one of mine. "I don't care about any of that."

"No, but I do. It's important to me to pay my way."

"Men are so dumb."

Her statement shocks me a little. Where once my little sister hung on my every word, this woman in front of me now speaks her mind.

"What?"

"The only thing I care about is you being here, out of prison. I don't care about the money. Renny, I just want you to be free. To do what you want when you want."

Slightly shaking my head, I say, "And I'm grateful to you, but I still need to pay my way."

"Fine. But you don't need to do it tonight." She hops off the chair. "Come on. Let's go eat."

My little sister listened.

Sure, Destiny is still asking me a million questions, but instead of some fancy restaurant, we are in a bar. It's the kind of place where the music is loud, and no one pays any mind to the people around them.

Kade, Destiny, and I are sitting in a booth at the back of the room. He let me sit facing the door so I could see any potential threats coming in. Kade understands me, at least a little.

A stocky guy walks into the bar. He looks around the room, spots me, and smiles. He's not someone I recognize. Walking toward us, I notice he's wearing a Savage Angels MC cut.

"We've got company."

Kade twists in the seat and shakes his head. "Bad company."

The guy reaches us and laughs. "The best fucking

company. Got room for one more?"

All eyes come to me.

"Ahh, sure?"

I get out of the booth, he slides in and holds out his hand. "Zeke Rushard."

"Rushard?" He nods. "Renny Bennett."

"Nice to meet you."

"You decided to take Rush's surname?" asks Kade, his eyebrows raised, seemingly surprised.

Zeke chuckles. "I'm testing it out."

"Are you and Rush a couple?"

Kade chokes on his beer, and Destiny shrieks with laughter.

"Ahh, no. I like vaginas. Rush is my father. Newly found." His brow furrows, and he appears a little pained. "It's a long story."

"Sorry, didn't mean to presume anything."

Zeke waves a hand in the air. "No harm, no foul." He picks up a menu. "Have you guys ordered?"

"Only drinks." Destiny picks up her glass and takes a sip.

"Dane and Kat might join us," states Zeke as he studies the menu.

"Should we get a bigger table?" Destiny asks Kade.

Kade shakes his head. "Let's wait to see if they come. Kat has been fickle lately."

"You like her?" I ask.

Kade picks up his beer and takes a swig. "Yeah,

she's good people, but the fans can be a pain in the ass. And now she's pregnant, she can't move as fast as she used to. It makes taking her out in public difficult."

"Judge never has a problem," Zeke says.

"Who's Judge?"

Kade raises his eyebrows and grins. "He's Kat's personal bodyguard around town. Judge is in the MC, and he's with Jasmin. She's also in The Grinders. Plays the keyboard and sings. Wild as a hellcat."

"Right. Didn't she have a baby not so long ago?"

Zeke nods. "Yep. It's Judge's. They're not married and have a weird relationship, but it works for them."

"Weird, how?"

"Jasmin spends a lot of time on the road. She leaves Noah with Judge." Zeke shakes his head. "Weird is the wrong word... I guess it's just not conventional. Normally, the woman takes care of the kid, but she's not built that way."

"Give me a break. Jasmin earns one hundred times more than what Judge earns. She travels a lot and doesn't have much of a maternal instinct, *but* she loves both of them. You get in her way, and she'll gut you. If she were a man, you'd be saying how good she is at bringing home the bacon."

The fire in Destiny's voice surprises me. I glance from her to Kade, who's grinning from ear to ear.

"Yep, just like you and me. You bring home the bacon, and I cook it."

Destiny giggles. "You have more money than me."

"You earn more than me."

Destiny's face goes soft, and she leans into his side.

"Stop. Renny and I are here alone. No kissing, no touching, and no mushy stuff."

"Jealous?" asks Kade.

"Oh, please." Zeke leans back.

"He is," Destiny agrees with Kade.

"Oh, fuck off. I have Cass."

Destiny laughs. "I'm only messing with you."

The waitress returns and asks, "Are you ready to order?"

The others tell her what they want. I'm the last to order, but I'm having a hard time deciding what I want.

Destiny reaches over and touches my hand. "You're up. What are you going to have?"

I glance up at the waitress, looking at me hopefully. "Ahh, I'm not sure. What's good?"

She smiles. "Everything. But how hungry are you?"

"Starving."

"Okay then, I'd go for the steak and ribs with a side of macaroni. It'll stick to your ribs, and I'd have the mashed potatoes and gravy for your other side."

"Okay."

"Okay?" I nod. "How do you want your steak cooked?"

"Medium."

"Great! Now, are you folks right for drinks?"

Zeke answers before anyone else, "Shiner Bock for me."

"I'll have the same."

Zeke lightly punches my arm. "Better than the imported shit Kade drinks, hey?"

Kade ignores him and orders a whiskey and a margarita with extra salt for Destiny.

"Okay, I'll be right back with some bread. Can I get you folks anything else?"

"We're good," answers Destiny.

The waitress walks away for only a minute and returns with two baskets of bread and different spreads. "I'm not supposed to give you more than one lot of bread, but it's going to be a while before the food comes out. If you need more, let me know." She winks at me and bustles away.

"She likes you." Zeke elbows my side.

"She's being polite and paid to flirt."

Destiny giggles. "Yep. Renny is right. The nicer she is, the more you'll tip. Doesn't mean she likes you… it's a job."

"I guess you'd know," Zeke replies. "But he was the only one she winked at."

"Maybe she likes tall men?" teases Kade.

"Fuck you, I'm almost six feet."

"And Renny is what, six-six, six-seven?" Kade grins.

"Six-seven." I chuckle. "And you know what they say, it's not the size, it's what you do with it."

Zeke smirks. "I think I've got it covered."

"All right, all right, keep it clean," orders Destiny.

"Do you still see Tobias?"

Destiny nods. "Yes, he keeps in touch. Occasionally, he'll drop into my work and say hi."

"You never told me that."

Destiny looks at Kade. "I'm sure I did."

"No. Not once have you said he's been to visit."

Destiny shrugs. "Well, now you know."

Kade turns his attention to me. "How do you know Tobias?"

"He came to visit me a couple of times. Wanted me to know he was taking care of Destiny."

"Did you know him before you went in?"

"Yeah, a little."

The waitress comes back with our drinks, and we eat the bread rolls and say nothing for a while, sitting in comfortable silence. The bar is loud with customers and music. I can see why Destiny loves Kade. It's the little things he does for her, like ordering her favorite drink, buttering her a bread roll, and putting an arm around her shoulders so she feels safe.

There was a time when I did all that for Thea.

Thea, the bitch who betrayed me.

"Renny?"

Raising my gaze, Destiny is staring at me.

"Yeah?"

"Have you thought about going back to the old neighborhood?"

"No," I say a little too quickly. "There's nothing for me there but bad memories."

Destiny searches my face. "You still have friends there."

"No, I don't. The only visitors I got were you and Tobias. There's no one there I need to see."

"Rush wants you to go back with him. He's going after the state to compensate you for the time you spent behind bars."

"Tell him not to."

Kade tilts his head to the side. "Why not? You went away for something you didn't do. Someone fucked up, and you deserve compensation for all those years."

"I only want to move on, forget it happened, and start from new."

"Yeah, but money will help all that happen," states Zeke.

"Money won't give me those years back."

Zeke nods, and a silent exchange occurs between him and Kade. Based on all that Destiny has shared with me, it's clear they've been friends for quite some time—likely the type of friendship that thrives without the need for words.

The waitress returns with more bread. “Sorry, folks, it shouldn’t be much longer.”

Not wanting to talk about my past, I change the subject. “So, when are you two getting married?”

Kade smiles at Destiny and squeezes her shoulder. “We were waiting on you. Destiny wanted to wait until you were out of prison.” He kisses her temple. “You need to pick a date, babe.”

“The sooner the better.” Destiny leans into Kade’s side. “I’ve got my dress. All we needed was for us to *all* be together.”

“Sounds good to me.” Kade kisses her again.

“Enough with the kissy, kissy. I’m best man, right?”

Kade frowns. “Best man?”

“Well, I am the *best* man for the job.”

Destiny giggles. “Renny, will you give me away?”

My eyebrows shoot up to my hairline. The idea of giving away Destiny doesn’t feel right. Kade locks eyes with me, and I feel Zeke’s eyes on me.

“Do you love my sister?”

“With all that I am.”

“Would you do anything for her?”

“*Anything*,” Kade answers forcefully.

My gaze travels to Destiny. “Is he the one?”

A smile creeps across her face. “Oh, yeah. He’s everything.”

Kade puts his forehead to the side of her face.

The way they treat each other is more than enough for me to have said yes, but hearing how each of them feels about the other, my answer is simple.

"I'd be honored to walk you down the aisle. But I'm not giving you away. Prison took away my time with you, and you've turned into a beautiful woman inside and out. I've missed so much. So, if you want me to walk you down the aisle, I will, but don't ask me to give you away."

Kade's steely blue eyes find mine. "You're not losing a sister, you're gaining a family." He raises his chin toward Zeke. "Zeke is family. The Savage Angels are family. You, Renny, are now part of that too. It's not only me you're getting… your family of two just became an army."

An army?

Interesting choice of words.

I wonder if he knows I'm going to go after my enemies and might need his *army* to help.

Raising my beer, I say, "To Kade and Destiny and my newfound family. May we all live happily ever after."

Destiny clinks her glass against mine. "I'll drink to that."

CHAPTER 2

THEA

The rain pours down as I dash for the subway. Overhead, lightning flashes, and I can't help but feel a sense of urgency. It's almost five o'clock, and rush hour seems even more chaotic than usual. I navigate through the crowd, dodging the puddles, and watch out for the occasional umbrella.

I'm already late for my second job. My boss will dock my pay and make a scene as soon as my rain-soaked ass makes it through the door. Jogging down the last few steps, I slip and land on my butt. While water seeps through my clothing, not one person stops to help as I scramble to my feet.

Great.

Just fucking *great.*

Limping a little, I make it to the platform, but my train has gone, so I'll need to wait for the next one.

Sighing, I look at the back of my pants, grateful they are black. Maybe no one will notice? My boss will, he's such a dick. I'd quit if I didn't need the money, but I've got bills.

Sitting on a seat, I pick up the newspaper next to me and flip through it. Then a familiar face stares back at me.

Renny.

The headline reads…

Renny Bennett - NOT GUILTY

My heart thuds quickly in my chest as I scan the article.

Every day for eight years, I've thought about Renny.

In the photograph, he's wearing a suit. The tattoos on his neck peek out, and he's sporting a beard—not a scruffy, long one, but one that's trimmed and kept short. Renny looks good. He's still handsome, but his eyes show aging. Even in this picture, you can tell he's been through a lot. The article says he's staying with his sister in Tourmaline until he gets settled.

"Can you believe they got him out?" says an older gentleman beside me.

"He didn't do it."

The old guy shakes his head. "Word is they're going to retry him."

"He didn't do it," I repeat.

I hold the newspaper up higher and hope the man gets the hint. Renny went to prison because of me and what I did.

I *know* he didn't do it.

Will he come searching for me?

I'll never forget the expression on his face the day he was sentenced. While he embraced his sister, his eyes locked onto mine. The intense loathing which filled his face as she wept in his arms shattered my heart.

Renny knew it was me.

Will it matter if I tell him I had no choice?

The urge to move again makes me groan. I've moved so many times in the past eight years—must be at least twenty. I really like the apartment building I'm in now. It's filled with good people and lots of families. Everyone looks out for each other. There's no crime, and I have a little garden growing on the fire escape. It feels like a sanctuary after so many moves.

The train stops. I take the newspaper and climb into the cramped car. Bodies are smushed together as we ride to our destinations. Thankfully, I only need to ride it for three stops, then run to the restaurant.

As soon as the doors open, I jog along the platform and up the stairs. The rain is still coming down, and I put the newspaper over my head. With my head down, I make my way through the crowd. I'm waiting for the crosswalk light to change color, minding my own business, when a hand lands on my shoulder. Spinning around and out of their grasp, I confront an old friend.

No, friend is the wrong word.

This is someone I never really knew.

"Hey, Thea, how goes it?"

"Hunter?" Scanning the immediate area, I don't see any of his friends, but with the rain and peak hour, they could be anywhere. "What do you want?"

"Did you see?"

Renny.

They've found me again to talk about Renny.

"I'm late for work."

"Yeah, you like working at Gino's? They say they have the best lasagna in town."

The light changes, and I jog across the road.

Once more, Hunter puts a hand on me, but this time, he spins me around. "Renny is out."

"And?" I ask, frustrated he's found me again.

His name suits him. All those times I've moved, Hunter has tracked me down. He and his buddies wanted me to know I'm easy to find and could hurt me whenever they wanted. They are bad news, and I wanted nothing to do with them in the first place. They were Renny's friends, not mine.

"Has he reached out?"

Hunter hasn't changed much over the years. He

has the same light brown hair, and the only sign he's getting older is the laugh lines around his pale blue eyes.

"Why would he?"

Hunter smirks. "Back in the day, he fell for you hard."

"That was eight years ago, and I don't know how many failed relationships. Renny isn't looking for me." There hasn't been anyone since Renny, but Hunter doesn't need to know.

Hunter pitches forward, his nose an inch from mine. "You'll let us know if he does? We'd hate for anything bad to happen to you or..."

Recoiling in fear and disgust as he draws nearer, I vehemently shake my head. "Renny won't ever come searching for me. He didn't even permit me to visit him in prison. Renny Bennett despises me because of my actions. Because of *you*."

"Not just me, Thea." He pulls out his phone and types. Within a couple of seconds, my phone dings. "You've got my number. You call me if he reaches out." His hand lashes out, and he grips my upper arm hard. "Remember what you have to lose."

Staggering backward, I pull out of his grasp. "Leave me alone," I hiss.

Hunter lets out a chuckle. "Still the same old Thea," he remarks, appraising me from head to toe, his gaze lingering on my chest. I feel my skin crawl under his intense scrutiny. "You're looking great.

Give me a call." With a laugh, he vanishes into the bustling crowd.

Rushing down the alleyway, I enter Gino's, grateful for the protection of people and to be out of the rain.

"What fucking time do you call this?" bellows Adrian.

"I call it late." My boss can be such a dick. "In case you haven't noticed, it's raining."

Adrian tosses a small hand towel at me. "Jesus, you look like a drowned rat. I'm docking your pay."

"I know."

Adrian moves closer to me. "What did you say?"

He has his hands on his hips and is staring at me like I'm something he needs to wipe off his perfectly polished shoes. If I didn't need this job, I'd tell him to stick it, but I'm a week late with the rent and every dollar counts.

"I said, I know, and I don't blame you. The rain sent everyone into the subway. I missed my train." I put the towel on my face and dab. "Give me a minute to clean up, and I'll be right out."

Adrian cocks his head to the side and nods. "Be quick about it."

Rushing past him, I enter the staff change room and open my locker. The newspaper is still clutched in my hand. Renny's picture is wet, and my throat closes as I stare at it. I put my backpack in the locker, place the paper on top, and head for the women's dressing room to see how bad I look in the mirror.

My hair is in a ponytail, and although wet, it's contained. Using Adrian's towel, I pat my hair down and wipe my face. My reflection in the mirror starkly contrasts with the photograph of Renny, who appears healthy and stronger than ever—I am too thin and in need of some sun. The dark circles under my eyes add years to my face. Pinching my cheeks to give myself some color, I hurry to the front of the restaurant. Adrian is seating a couple and glances at another couple over by the wall. This is his way of telling me to serve them.

Plastering a smile on my face, I walk over to them. "Hello, welcome to Gino's. I'm Thea. Would you like a drink to start?"

They smile up at me and place their order.

Little did I know this would be the beginning of a long shift as people file in to avoid the rain and have someone else make their dinner.

It's nearly midnight by the time the last customer leaves. I'm clearing their table when Adrian comes to stand beside me.

"You did good tonight."

"We were busy."

"Yeah." He puts his hands in his pockets and rocks back on his heels.

"Do you want something, Adrian?"

"You've been late three times in the last month."

Standing up straighter, I face him. "And I've had a good excuse each time. Adrian, I'm the best waitress you've got. I work twice as hard as the others, do extra work in the kitchen to help, and I'm good at this job." My eyes drop to his chest as tears threaten to fall. "Dock my pay, but Adrian, I really do need this job."

He grunts and turns away. "See you tomorrow. Don't be late. I've left your tips in your locker."

Relieved, I finish clearing the table and walk into the kitchen, where the crew is finishing up for the night.

"Night, fellas."

They mumble their goodbyes as I walk to the staff room. Opening my locker, there's an envelope on top of the newspaper. I stuff it and the newspaper into my backpack and head for the back entrance.

The train journey takes forty-five minutes, and once I get off, my apartment is only a block away. Assuming I catch the train, I should be home by one fifteen.

The rain has stopped as I jog toward the subway.

There are not many people around at this hour, and I give a wide berth to those who are. The lights in the subway station flicker on and off, painting the entire area in a creepy yellow light. My train is on time, and because it's so late, there's hardly anyone in the car. I sit for the first time in hours, and the relief to my feet is instant. They pulse as the blood flows through them.

It's been a weird day. Opening my bag, I pull out the newspaper and reread the article on Renny Bennett. I study the picture of him again and wonder if he's even thought of me over the years. With a sigh, I put the newspaper back in my bag. If Hunter has found me, it means the others know where I am too. The thought of moving makes me feel physically ill.

Closing my eyes, I weigh up my options. It's doubtful Renny will come looking for me. I wrote to him every week the first year he was in prison, but the letters came back to me unopened. There were so many conversations I wanted to have with him to explain why I did what I did. One thing I know for sure is Renny will never forgive me.

The train lurches to a stop, and my eyes fly open. I must have dozed off. It's my stop. On weary legs, I stand and walk the short distance to my apartment.

The door opens before I get to it, and Mia is smiling. "Girl, you look awful."

Mia lives next door with her younger brother

and is a good friend.

"Thanks," I whisper. "Was everything okay?"

Mia nods. "Little man went down after I read the same story three times." She chuckles. "He sure has a fascination with motorbikes, doesn't he?"

"Yes. He's been watching ATVs on YouTube. Keeps telling me he's going to get one when he's older."

Mia reaches out and touches my arm. "Girl, you better get to bed. You working tomorrow?"

"Aren't I always?"

She searches my face and says, "No rest for the wicked."

I belt out a laugh. "When do I have time to get wicked?"

Mia raises her eyebrows and says, "Girl, a man knocking on your door tonight?"

My heart sinks. "A man?"

"Yeah, tall, a bit of a looker."

"Did he leave a name?"

"Hunter."

Fuck.

Mia steps closer to me. "From the expression on your face, he isn't a friend. He knew Zachary's name."

"He's someone from my past I'd rather forget. If he comes by again, don't let him in."

"An old boyfriend?"

I cringe at the thought. "No. Absolutely, no. Just

someone I'd rather never see again."

"Should I call the police if he comes by again?"

I want to say yes, but Hunter hasn't technically done anything this time, and I don't want to worry Mia.

Shaking my head, I say, "You ever had a friend from your past you were done with? Like someone who never grew up or moved on, but they sorta got stuck in the life they were dealt? That's Hunter. I moved on a long time ago, but he's still playing the bad boy and..."

"And you've got Zach and have no time for bullshit or lowlifes?"

Smiling, I say. "Yeah."

"Okay, well, if he comes by again, I'll call Tyrone to escort him out of the building. He'll get the hint really quick. Now, go shower and sleep. What time do you start in the morning?"

"I need to be up by six and out the door by seven."

"Want me to walk Zach to school?"

Throwing my arms around her, I squeeze her tight. "What would I do without you?"

Mia hugs me tightly. "Maybe not work so much?"

It's true. Without Mia to look after Zachary, I wouldn't be able to work as much as I do. But it also means we'd be in a worse neighborhood, and Zachary would be at a different school.

He loves the school he's at now.

Letting her go, I reach into my bag and pull out the envelope with my tips in it. Mia's hands close over mine.

"Nope. You can buy me a coffee on your next day off. Girl, you keep that."

"No, that's not the deal."

"Well, I'm changing the deal. Besides, I saw you're past due with some bills. You can pay me when you're caught up."

Tears prick the backs of my eyelids. "No, it's okay, really."

I love Mia and appreciate her trying to give me some breathing room, but a deal is a deal. With her taking care of Zachary, I already feel like I'm imposing on our friendship. Paying my way is a matter of pride.

Pulling out a few notes, I thrust them at her. "You take this. You need it too."

Mia screws her lips to one side but eventually takes the money. "You're a hard woman."

"Nah." I smile. "Thanks for everything. See you in the morning."

"My pleasure and girl… it *is* morning."

Mia walks the short distance to her apartment, and I shut the door. Walking into my bedroom, I drop my bag on the floor and fall onto my bed. Sleep is calling my name, but I have things to do before I can close my eyes. Sitting up, I strip out of my clothes and put on an old T-shirt—it comes to my knees. Zachary's door is open, and I stick my head in to check on him. He's lying on his stomach, one arm hanging off the bed, and his little mouth is slightly open. I pull the blankets up and over him and kiss the side of his face.

Returning to my room, I pick up my clothes and take them into the bathroom. I have plenty of white shirts, but only one pair of good black pants. Turning on the sink's faucet, I make it nice and hot and wash them. When I'm done, I hang them over a chair in the dining room and face the pedestal fan on them so I know they will be dry by morning. Returning to the bathroom, I take a long, hot shower, wash my hair, and let the water ease my tired muscles. To keep my hair a little respectable, I braid it. Lastly, I smother my face in a night cream and crawl into bed.

The clock says seven minutes past two.

Groaning, I lay on my bed, close my eyes, and drift off to old memories of Renny.

"Mom!"

Cracking an eyelid, I stare at my son. "What?"

"Your alarm has been going off for ten minutes."

Sitting up, I hit the off button—the clock reads six thirty.

Dammit.

I'm so tired it feels like I only just went to sleep.

"Okay, you make us breakfast while I get ready."

Zachary smiles. "Already did it. Pop-Tarts are waiting for you in the bathroom."

Ruffling his hair, I say, "Thanks, honey. Mia is going to walk you to school."

"You can't?"

"No, I've got an early start today."

His little face bunches up, but he doesn't say anything. Zachary nods and walks out of the room. I've got three more days of work before I get a day off. I was going to ask if I could work, but my son needs to spend some time with me.

Hustling into the bathroom, I wash my face, eat my Pop-Tarts, and then put on makeup. The braids kept my blonde hair under control. Brushing it out, it falls in waves and, for once, doesn't look bad. I hit it with hairspray then walk into the living room. Zachary is sitting on the couch, dressed for school and watching television.

"Did you do your homework?"

"Yes, ma'am."

"What do you want for lunch?" I sit beside him and put my socks on.

"Made myself a PBJ."

He's growing up so fast. Maybe too fast.

"Fruit?"

"We don't have any."

"Muesli bar?"

He shakes his head. "Ate the last one yesterday."

"I'll give you money. Ask Mia to stop and get you something on the way to school."

"It's okay, Mom."

"A PBJ isn't enough to eat."

His lips turn down at the corners. "Okay."

Walking back into my bedroom, I pick up my bag, pull out the newspaper, put it on my dresser, then carry it back to the couch. Opening the envelope, I pull out my tips. There are two hundred dollars in small bills. Last night's patrons must have tipped big. I hold out twenty dollars to Zachary.

"Here, don't buy junk."

"I won't."

"I mean it." Standing, I touch my black pants, and they're almost dry, but I need to wear them, so I put them on anyway. "I'll try to buy some groceries between jobs, okay?"

"Okay. We need milk and bread."

Jesus.

I'm failing this kid big time.

We don't even have the basics.

"Gotcha." Leaning down, I kiss the top of his head. "Love you to the moon and back."

"Love you too, Mom."

"Have fun at school."

"I will."

"See you tomorrow."

"Can I stay up and see you?"

I put my backpack on. "It's a school night, buddy."

"Come on, Mom. I'm nearly ten."

Giggling, I say, "Hmm… that's a stretch."

"Well, I will be in a couple of years."

"And in a couple of years, we'll talk about it."

Zachary pouts, but he doesn't argue.

"Mind Mia and have a good day."

"Okay."

Leaning down again, I kiss the top of his head and then move for the door. When I open it, Hunter is outside, leaning against the opposite wall.

Quickly, I close it behind me. "What are you doing here?" I hiss.

"Did he call?"

"Who? Renny? No!"

Hunter squints at me and finally nods. "I believe you."

"Fuck you. Don't you come here ever again. Renny isn't interested in me. He's not going to call or visit or…" Words fail me as I stare at Hunter.

"Maybe not you, but what about the kid?"

"He doesn't know."

Hunter barks out a laugh. "Sure, he doesn't."

Straightening my shoulders, I pull myself up to

my full height of five-foot-five. "He wouldn't see me. Renny wouldn't even read my letters. He. Doesn't. Know."

Hunter's eyes go wide as he grins down at me. "You're not fucking lying, are you?"

Frustrated, I throw my hands in the air. "I'm late. Can we move this outside?"

Hunter stares at my closed door for a heartbeat, then walks ahead of me down the hallway to the elevator. I stab the button forcefully, the doors open, and we both get in. He says nothing on the ride down to the ground floor. The doors open, and I step out of the elevator and keep walking until I hit the sidewalk.

Turning on him, I put one hand on my hip and poke the air in front of him. "Keep away from me and my son."

Hunter glances up at the building and then back at me. "You'll let me know if Renny calls?"

"He *won't* call."

"Yeah, but if he does?"

Frustrated, I suck in a deep breath and release it slowly. "Yes. Okay? Yes! But he's not going to call. He has no reason to call."

Hunter crosses his arms over his chest and smiles. "Revenge is a powerful reason to find you."

"Do you really think he wants to see *me* after eight years in prison?"

Hunter leans in and, with a threatening voice, says, "Do you *really* think after eight years in prison, he's thought about anything else *other* than getting even? Renny was a hard man before he went to jail. What do you think he's like now?"

Words get caught in my throat as I remember Renny. Where once he would have defended me with his last breath, now he'd probably turn away if I were on fire. Hell, he'd likely add fuel to the fire to watch me burn.

Hunter smirks. "Seems like you and Zach have a nice life. It'd be a shame to fuck it all up because of Renny Bennett. If we go down, we're taking you and your son with us."

My heart skips a beat.

Since the day this mess all started, it's been the same threat. They keep going after my son, and I'm tired of it. Tired of them.

But there's no one to protect me or to turn to, so I do what I've always done. I nod, agree, and wish to God they'd all disappear. And sometimes I wish I'd never met Renny Bennett, but immediately I take it back because I wouldn't have Zachary without him.

"If he calls, I'll reach out," I say through gritted teeth.

Hunter tilts his head slightly, then turns and walks away.

I watch him disappear around a corner, then

look at my watch.

Shit!

I'm going to be late.

CHAPTER 3

RENNY

Kade had some unfinished business in LA. Destiny insisted I tag along for the ride. Being around my kid sister and her fiancé, I now understand the term *third wheel* more than I ever wanted to.

They're inside a bank. It turns out Kade is worth a pretty penny. According to Destiny, it's old money from his mother's side of the family. I'm waiting outside, enjoying the warm sun on my face.

I crack my eyes and see the love birds walking toward me. Destiny is happy. It radiates out of her very soul.

Pushing off the car, I ask, "All good?"

"Yeah, Renny, all good. What do you want to do?" Destiny moves to the passenger side, and I hustle to open her door.

"I'm easy."

"Well, I want to go to all the touristy places. Kade, you can be our guide."

Kade smiles at her, but he groans as soon as the door closes. "I'm never going to get her home, am I?"

"Nope. My little sister has stars in her eyes. It's Hollywood, baby."

Kade laughs, and I try to give him a sympathetic look, but I'm pretty sure I'm grinning like the cat who swallowed the canary.

Kade opens the driver's side door, and I'm about to open the passenger door when a loud, angry voice says, "Renny Bennet, is that you?"

Fuck.

I do a double take on the man, then point at Kade. "*Drive.* Drive now."

Thankfully, Kade doesn't need to be told twice, and before I have my door shut, he's peeling out of the parking space and into traffic.

"Who was that?" Kade demands, staring at me in the rearview mirror.

"Old friend."

"Friend or enemy?"

"Did I miss something?" Destiny twists in the seat to look at me.

"It's nothing."

"Nah, don't do that. Your sister isn't some dainty female who can't take care of herself. She's been doing fine on her own while you were in prison, and now she has me. Don't you dare say it's nothing."

Destiny nods once. "Damn straight!" Her eyes lock with mine. "What the fuck is going on?"

Part of me is angry at having to explain myself, but a greater part of me is proud of her for demanding to know the truth.

"I have enemies. Being in prison for so long, I owe a lot of people favors. The guy back there was in with me at Glenford. He's probably wondering why I haven't repaid my debt."

"Why haven't you?" asks Kade.

"Can we talk about this later?" I glance at Destiny.

"Oh, no. We're not doing that. You're not doing the big macho bullshit thing where the little woman gets to sit in the dark and not get told a thing. You tell me what the fuck is going on, and you tell me now. You *owe me*, brother."

"I owe you?" I ask incredulously.

"Yes! Do you know how many sleepless nights I endured? You were my soul focus for eight fucking years, and I'm not losing you to some asshole who believes you owe him a debt." A single tear tracks down her pretty face. "I love you, Renny, and you owe me. You owe me time and, and... I want to get to know you again. I've missed you." She twists back around in the seat and faces forward.

Kade grips the steering wheel so tightly his knuckles turn white. They are silent as I search for the right words.

"Destiny, I'm sorry. And you're right, I owe you. Getting to know you and the life you've made, well, it's something I want to do. But I owe some people, and, D, some people owe me."

Her head drops to her chest, and her shoulders move up and down as though she's breathing heavily.

"If you live by the sword, you'll die by it."

Staring at the back of her head, I say, "I have no intention of dying."

Destiny turns to look at me. "How can we help?"

Her words surprise me.

"It's not something I want you involved in."

Destiny's gaze flicks to Kade and then back to me. "Fine, I'll stay out of it, but Kade and the Savage Angels can help. And maybe if you get your head out of your ass, you'll let them."

Kade nods, then reaches over and places his hand on her shoulder. "Your sister is smart. You should listen to her."

Here I am wanting to protect my little sister when it's not my job anymore. I guess it hasn't been for a long time.

Releasing a breath, I sit forward in my seat and put my elbows on my knees. "I have a list."

Kade shows understanding by dipping his chin to his chest. "How many?"

"Six names."

"Are they the reason you ended up in jail?"

With my lips turning down in a sneer, I say, "Yes."

"Who?" whispers Destiny.

"Thea North, Jackson MacKenzie, Steve Plant, Hunter Johns, Samuel Perth, and Derrick Long." The names I've held inside me for so long fall from my lips, and relief washes through me at sharing my burden.

"Thea?" asks Destiny as she turns once again to face me.

"Yeah."

"I remember her. She phoned me a bunch of times after you went to prison. Thea was your girl."

I huff out a laugh. "Yeah. *My girl.* She's the one who sent me into the room with three dead bodies. Thea was the reason I was there in the first place."

"Oh, Renny. I didn't know."

"No one knew. Those names I recited? They were once in my inner circle. Each one of them played a part in getting me locked up."

Kade pulls the car over. "Why'd they turn on you?"

"Money."

Kade's lips get into a hard line. He stares at my sister then back at me. "Who do you owe?"

"That list is a lot shorter. There are three men I owe favors. The guy we just left, his name is Brandon Wills. The other two are still in prison, so their favors can wait."

"Can Wills wait?" asks Kade.

"I'll smooth things over with him. He's probably pissed I haven't reached out since I got out."

"You only just got out." Destiny reaches between the seats and takes my hand. "Surely, he'll understand?"

"What does he want?"

My eyes flick to Kade. "He has a problem with a loan shark who's involved with the Abruzzi Crime Family."

Destiny lets go of my hand and looks at Kade. "Could Sal help?"

"Sal?" I ask.

"Salvatore Agostino."

My eyes bug out, and my mouth drops open. "You know Salvatore Agostino?"

Destiny shrugs. "Yes. He's married to Dane's sister, Emily. They visit once in a while with their kids."

"You're serious?"

Destiny's gaze pivots from Kade to me, a crease forming between her brows. "Yes. He's a good guy."

I bark out a laugh. "He's anything but a good guy. Salvatore Agostino is a captain in the Abruzzi Crime Family. He's ruthless. Jesus, D, the man is a killer."

Kade shakes his head. "Not for us. Sal is known for getting things done, but he's family. He can help."

"Yeah, but at what cost? I don't want to owe the Abruzzis' anything."

"Not the Abruzzis'... Sal. We'll set up a meeting. Tell him your problem, and we'll see if he can help."

My eyebrows go up in surprise. "You're going to call Salvatore Agostino on your phone and set up a meet? Just like that?"

Kade pulls his cell out of his pocket. "Yep, I've got him in my contacts. We can do it now if you like?"

"Fuck off." Leaning back in the seat, I stare at the two of them. "You're serious?"

"Sal is family," Destiny repeats Kade's sentiments.

"Do you work for him?"

Destiny shakes, then nods her head. "Sort of? He's purchased a house in Tourmaline, and I helped with the contracts. Other than that, no."

"You don't want to work with the mob," I state.

"As opposed to working with the Savage Angels? Jesus, Renny, judgmental much?" Destiny faces forward in her seat.

Kade cocks his head to the side. "You need to learn how to trust. I get it... your old crew did you wrong, but no one in our inner circle would ever do that to you."

Kade turns, puts the indicator on, and pulls the car back into traffic. No one speaks as he drives back to the hotel. When the car is parked, we all climb out.

Learning to trust isn't going to come easily for me. My friends were my world, and I would have done anything for them. It never occurred to me they would betray me. I honestly don't know if I can trust like that again.

"I'm going to go up to the room." Destiny kisses Kade's cheek. "See you both later."

Kade watches her walk away and then gestures toward the bar in the hotel. "Let's talk."

He chooses a chair away from the few people here, and I settle into the seat facing him.

"How was this Wills going to get you to help?"

Searching his face, I try to decide if he can be trusted. So far, he's done nothing for me to mistrust him. My sister is in love with him, and he's gone out of his way to make me feel welcome.

"He probably wanted to use me as muscle to intimidate."

"Maybe worse?"

Knowing Wills like I do, murder wouldn't be off the table. "Maybe."

"And you'd do it to settle your debt?"

"You ever been locked up, Kade? To stay alive, I would have done a deal with the devil himself," I snarl. "So, yeah, I owe Wills, and I repay my debts, but there are things I need to do first."

Kade holds up a finger as a server approaches.

"What can I get for you two?"

"Whiskey," states Kade.

"Anything in particular?"

"Glen Grant… the older, the better."

"And you, sir?"

"Beer, whatever is on tap."

She walks away, and he steeples his fingers together on the table. His hair falls across his face, hiding one eye.

"Sal can help. There's no need for you to get your hands dirty."

"Wills won't see it that way."

"Fuck Wills. You don't need to tell him how you got it done, only that it is done. Sure, Sal will want something in return, but it won't be murder."

"I've been locked up for eight years. I've got nothing to trade with."

"You have me, your sister, and if you let them, the Savage Angels can help."

"Why would you help me?"

"You're not getting it, are you? Destiny is part of my family now, and that family includes the Savage Angels. By default, you're in too." He crosses his arms across his chest. "But if you fuck us over, I'll drive you to the barn myself, and Destiny will never know what happened to you."

"Did you threaten me?"

"Not a threat, a promise."

He pushes his hair out of his face so I can see his steel-blue eyes. There's no humor in them, and his mouth is set in a hard line.

"Set up the meet. But not yet. There are things I have to do first."

Kade uncrosses his arms. "Who's first?"

"Thea."

"Do you know where she is?"

"No, but she won't be hard to find."

"One of the brothers is a computer wizard. Give me her name and date of birth... he'll track her down."

He has no reason to help me. Sure, I'm his girl's brother, but it doesn't mean he owes me a damn thing. Yet here he is, offering to help and bringing the power of his club with him.

"Does Dane know?"

Kade smiles. "He knows you need help. Told me to tell you not to bring trouble to his house, but if you needed help, we are to extend a hand."

"Is this all because of Destiny?"

Kade's eyes soften. "She's part of it. Destiny went through a bad patch a while back. The club feels responsible for her."

"Bad patch?"

Kade's lips turn down. "Not for me to tell. If Destiny wants you to know, she can tell you."

From the way he's talking, it sounds like Destiny was hurt. But from the little I know of him, I know he won't tell me more. There's so much I need to know, and so much I don't want Kade, Destiny, and the Savage Angels to be associated with.

"Destiny never needs to know your secrets, Renny. It's why she went up to the room. She only wants you to share as much with her as you want."

"My sister is smarter than I think she is."

Kade chuckles. "Yep."

The server returns and puts down napkins before placing our drinks on the table. "Enjoy."

Kade throws back his drink and stands. "What's Thea's full name and date of birth?"

"I'll text it to you."

"Good. I'm going to go check on Destiny."

With that, he strides out of the bar and leaves me to wonder if maybe, just maybe, I can trust him and the Savage Angels.

CHAPTER 4

RENNY

Whoever Kade contacted in the Savage Angels, it took him less than an hour to track down Thea. The next day, Kade rented me a car, and now I'm sitting across from her apartment building, waiting to glimpse her. He programmed his number, Dane's, and Zeke's into my cell phone and said to call if I needed anything. It's strange for me to have people do things for me and not want something in return.

Thea's apartment building is in a nice part of town. It's near a park. Sitting straighter in my seat, I watch as she approaches on the opposite side of the street. Her blonde hair is pulled back in a ponytail. She's not wearing makeup, and despite being too thin, Thea seems happy. When we were together, she always wore makeup, and her long hair was always curled. Maybe she's not so worried about her looks anymore. I never thought she needed all that crap on her face, but she seemed to think she did. Perhaps she's changed?

She's waving to someone further down the street. I watch as a boy runs to her, and she wraps her arms around him. They both laugh, then he immediately pulls out of her grasp and checks to see if anyone is watching. Thea ruffles his hair, and he pats it back down.

They're talking, and Thea nods. From my position, I can't hear the conversation. The kid hugs her again and crosses the road near where I'm sitting.

He stops and cups his hand over his mouth. "Mom!" My eyes go to Thea. "One or two?"

She holds up two fingers and keeps walking.

The boy passes my car and stares at me.

My heart thuds loudly in my chest.

He's got my eyes.

The boy breaks eye contact and continues on his way. I watch him in the side mirror until he disappears around a corner. Pulling my cell out of my pocket, I dial Kade.

"Is everything okay?" Kade asks.

"She has a son."

"And?"

"He looks like me, and he could be the right age."

"I'll get Guru to investigate. It's what he does best."

"Don't tell Destiny."

"Wasn't going to, brother."

Kade ends the call, and I search for Thea, but she's no longer on the street.

Starting the car, I drive away.

It never occurred to me Thea could have been pregnant.

Is he mine?

Does it change anything?

My immediate thought is *no.*

But...

Kade rented me a room in a cheaper motel. Not a dive, but not five stars like he and Destiny seem to enjoy staying in. I'm keeping a mental tally of all the money I owe them, but it weighs on me how much they're spending. I need to pay my way and take care of myself. His computer wizard, Guru, says the boy's name is Zachary. The dates match up to my incarceration, but why didn't she tell me?

The next day, I'm waiting outside Thea's apartment on the opposite side of the road. This time, I'm going to talk to her. I'm wearing jeans, a black T-shirt, and a denim jacket. People stare at me as they pass. I have a lot of tattoos, and the ones on my neck often make passersby do a double take.

Thea comes out, and the boy is with her. He runs ahead as I cross the street. Thea looks up at me approaching and freezes.

"Renny?" Her voice is breathy.

"Hello, Thea."

When I am in front of her, she glances toward her son and then steps back.

"You shouldn't be here."

"Is Zachary mine?"

Her hand flies to her mouth, and she shakes her head. "No."

"Sure looks like me, and the dates seem to match up."

"He's not yours."

"Who's is he then?"

"He's mine."

Her pretty hazel eyes seem scared. She's wearing her hair down today and looks tired. Her eyes appear older like they've seen too much.

"Who's the father?"

Thea shakes her head and jogs after her son. "He's mine."

Striding after her, I reach out and grab her arm. Thea flinches as though I'm going to hit her, and I instantly let her go. She stumbles and falls on her ass.

"Jesus, Thea."

I hold out a hand to her, but she's still shaking her head and scrambling to get away from me. "You can't be here." Thea looks around quickly. "They'll know. Please, Renny, just go. Leave me in the past."

"Like you did to me when you set me up?"

Her face turns white, and she visibly recoils at my accusation. She awkwardly gets to her feet and puts some distance between us. It takes a moment, but she squares her shoulders and meets my gaze. "He's not yours."

Closing the gap, I step into her personal space. "Who'd you fuck when we were together?" I ask through gritted teeth.

"It doesn't matter. It was a long time ago. Please, Renny, if you ever felt anything for me, leave us alone. I'm so sorry for what happened to you, I truly am, but it wasn't my fault."

Her eyes drop to my chest, but I see the pain in them. This woman was the one person I thought I'd spend the rest of my life with. It was only her. An ache tears through my chest as I stare down at her. I wish time had taken a toll on her, but she's prettier now than she was nearly a decade ago.

"Mom, are you coming?"

Zachary is standing a short distance from us.

I step back from his mother and give him a two-fingered wave. "Hey, Zachary. I'm Renny."

He marches toward me and holds out his hand. "Hello." He glances up at his mother. "Do you work with my mom?"

Zachary positions himself in front of his mother, and I'm impressed he shook my hand.

"Your mom and I are old friends."

He turns toward his mother. "Another one?"

Thea puts her arms around him and pulls him into herself. She smiles down at him. "Yeah, honey, seems like they're coming out of the woodwork."

Putting my hands in my pockets, I scan her neighborhood. No one is paying us any attention. When I look back at Thea, she's doing the same thing.

"Has your mom had many old friends visiting her lately?"

Zachary nods. "Just one, his name was Hunter."

My eyebrows move to my hairline. "Hunter Johns?"

Zachary shrugs a shoulder up to his ear. "Not sure."

Thea moves him back, smiling widely at the boy. "Honey, why don't you hurry along to the park? I'll be along shortly. Give me a minute to catch up with Renny, okay?"

"You won't be long?"

"No, honey."

"It was nice to meet you, Renny."

"You too, Zachary."

"My friends call me Zach." He smiles at me and runs toward what I assume is the park.

I watch him go, and when I redirect my attention back to Thea, she's examining me closely.

"You did good with him."

"I had to. It's only the two of us."

"Why didn't you tell me?"

Thea shakes her head and fast walks after her son. "He's not your responsibility."

Shouting after her, I say, "We're not done, Thea. I'll be back."

Thea doesn't turn around, but she does quicken her pace.

Today did not go as I thought it would, and after meeting Zachary, I know he's mine.

CHAPTER 5

THEA

Seeing Renny was a huge shock to my system. He's older and has more tattoos than before. But he's still the same, demanding and sexy as hell. Things are different for me. I have Zachary now, and I'm not the same young woman who fell for all of Renny's promises.

Zachary is in his room, finishing an art project. Renny used to like to draw. Lord knows Zachary didn't get his artistic ability from me. Even the stick figures I try to draw are embarrassing.

A knock sounds on my door, and for a brief moment, I hope it's Renny. Rushing to open it, unfortunately, it's Hunter. I try to slam the door closed, but he pushes his way in.

"You didn't call, Thea."

I keep moving backward until my back hits the

living room wall. Hunter places a hand on either side of my head and leans in. He licks his lips and peers down at my chest. "Why didn't you call, Thea?"

"Renny was here."

"We know." He moves his face closer to mine. "It was hours ago, and you didn't call."

"H-he wanted to know about Zachary."

Hunter presses himself against me, and I turn my head away from him. "And what did you tell him? Did you tell him about us? Did you tell him how we all conspired to put him in jail?" Hunter licks the side of my face, and I gag.

"Get off me."

"What did you tell him, hmm?"

"Mom?"

Hunter pushes himself off me. "Hey, there, little man. Your mommy was telling me about an old friend who came to visit today. Did you meet him?"

"Do you mean Renny?"

Hunter grins, and my flesh crawls. Shuffling past him, I put my hands on Zachary's shoulders and herd him toward his bedroom. "Sweetie, why don't you finish up your art project? Let Mommy catch up with…" I hesitate as I search for the right words. "Ahh… Hunter."

"Okay." Zachary looks at me, concern in his eyes. "I only need to sign it, and it's done."

"I won't be long."

He nods in my direction and casts Hunter one final glance before returning to his room.

"Leave now." I turn around and face the bastard. "Leave now, or I swear I'll scream this place down."

Hunter smirks and pulls back his jacket, revealing a gun. "Go ahead. We'll see who makes the most noise."

"I didn't tell him anything. Renny asked about Zachary. He didn't even mention you."

Hunter narrows his eyes and tilts his head to one side. "If you're lying—"

"I'm not."

Hunter looks me up and down, then walks backward toward my door. "Next time you see him, you call me, Thea. You've got it good here." He opens the door. "You and the boy have a good life… I'd hate to see anything happen to the two of you."

Hunter walks out, and I hurry to close and lock the door. He's right about one thing—I do have a good life here, but it's over now. They'll never leave me alone for fear of what I might tell Renny. Walking into my bedroom, I pick up the newspaper with the article about Renny. His sister, Destiny, lives in Tourmaline. Renny might not love me anymore, but family is everything to him. When I admit Zachary is his son, he'll protect him, and that's all I care about.

Reaching under the bed, I pull out my old blue suitcase and begin throwing clothes into it.

"Mom?"

Zachary is standing in the doorway with a crease between his eyebrows, looking confused.

"Honey, go pick out a week's worth of clothes. We're going on a road trip."

"We are? What about school?"

Smiling broadly, I shake my head. "Early vacation. I'll let them know."

"But, Mom, it's not vacation time for ages. I don't want to miss school."

"It won't be for long, I promise. Mommy needs to visit with an old friend and make sure we're safe."

"Safe?"

"Shit." I tilt my head from side to side, give him big eyes, and laugh. "Wrong word. You know how tired I get!" I hit myself up the side of my head. "Remember Renny we met today?"

"Yeah?"

"Well, he has a home in a beautiful part of the country, and he invited us to stay for a little while. Just a quick visit. You'll catch up on school. Now, go pack."

"Only a week?"

"Yes, honey, one week."

His lips turn down, and I can tell he doesn't believe me, but he does as he's told. Rushing into the bathroom, I put our toiletries into a plastic bag and throw them into the suitcase. Being tidy isn't high on my priorities right now. Getting Zachary out of here and somewhere safe is my only thought.

There's no way Hunter and the others aren't going to come back. They can't risk me telling Renny what I know.

Even if I tell Renny, he'll never forgive me.

He trusted me, and I betrayed him.

The only difference between Renny and my old friends is Renny might kill me, but he'd never hurt his son.

The others—they will kill us both.

It took a train trip, two buses, and three days to get to Tourmaline. Just in case we were being followed, I took longer than normal to get here. If we'd driven, not that I have a car, it would have taken a day.

Zachary knows something is wrong, and after the first day, he became quiet. He wanted to call his friends and art teacher, but I said no. My son knows when we're running, although it took him a little while to figure out we're doing it again.

He's mad at me, and I don't blame him. Before, when we've had to move, I explained why. This time, I didn't.

How do I tell him we stayed too long in that apartment building with Mia?

How do I tell him it's all my fault we must move again?

Jesus, help me.

How do I tell him we are going to see his father?

The father I've never allowed him to know. The father I refused to give him any information about for fear he'd want to see him.

The first rays of dawn are peeking over the mountains as we step off the bus at a quarter past five in the morning. At this early hour, the streets are nearly deserted, with only a few merchants preparing for the day ahead. My eyes catch on a cozy café called 'Betty's,' where a man is placing a hand-painted sign out the front as we drive by.

Taking a deep breath, the crisp morning air is scented with pine and possibilities. As I look around, the main street is lined with charming mom-and-pop shops rather than big chain stores. It's a quaint mountain town nestled snugly in a wide valley and surrounded on all sides by looming peaks and slopes dotted with evergreens. It's not hard to imagine how scenic this spot likely becomes when blanketed in snow during the winter months. For now, though, it brims with small-town charm and fresh starts.

Smiling at Zachary, I ask, "You hungry?"

"Yes, ma'am."

He avoids meeting my gaze, and it breaks my heart. Zachary is angry with me, and I don't blame him. It's not easy for a kid to start a new school and make new friends. This last time, he did so well—we did so well. Zachary had friends, a school he loved, and a safe place to live. Even I was doing better. And now, because of my actions, we have to start all over again.

"Come on, little man. Let's go eat."

As we cross the street and approach the café, a tall, muscular man steps forward and holds the door open.

"After you," he offers with a polite smile.

He seems vaguely familiar, though I'm certain I don't know him since I've never set foot in this town before. I return a gracious smile and step inside, Zachary following close on my heels.

The interior of the café is a charming throwback to the 1950s. The black and white checkered tile floor contrasts sharply with the bright red upholstered booths lining the walls and windows. A gleaming counter stretches nearly the length of the space, stools tucked neatly underneath. Smaller tables occupy the remaining area. Despite its retro appearance, the place has a cozy, welcoming vibe.

"Hey, Dane. You here for the usual?"

"Yes, please, Howie. Kat had a rough night. Your apple pie seems to be the only thing that doesn't upset her."

The young man behind the counter laughs before shifting his gaze toward me. "Please seat yourself wherever you'd like. Can I get you a cup of coffee to start?"

"Yes, please."

He smiles and turns over a mug, pouring hot coffee into it. "You sure are in here early. The grill is on, but it'll take a minute for everything to heat up. Did you come in on the bus?"

I nod.

"Howie, pour me one too, please?" the tall man asks.

"Sure, Dane."

Howie glances at me. "Milk? Sugar?"

"Both."

He then directs his attention to Zachary. "How about you? What can I get you?"

Zachary looks up at me. "Is it okay?"

"He'll have a chocolate milk."

"I make a mean hot chocolate," replies Howie with a grin.

"Mom?"

"Sure, honey."

Zachary chooses a booth near the window, and I take my coffee from Howie. "His hot chocolate will only be a minute."

"Thank you."

Dane smiles down at me. "So, you got off the bus?" I nod. "Have you got family here?"

"Yes."

I don't elaborate. Instead, I sit opposite Zachary and sip my coffee.

"I know just about everybody in town. Who are you here to see?"

"An old friend."

"I thought you said you were here to visit family?"

This guy won't give me a break.

I'm mentally trying to figure out how much money I have left, which isn't a lot—maybe enough to buy Zachary breakfast and dinner, but I'm going to have to go without.

"It's complicated." I offer him a smile, then look at Zachary.

I can feel his eyes on me, but he doesn't bother me further. He sits on a stool and stares out the window. Howie called the behemoth who wants to know everything, Dane. I guess he's one of those nosey small-town men you read about in books.

The bell over the door sounds, and a man walks in, shaking his head at Dane. "You're up early, Prez. Is our girl okay?"

He's clad in faded jeans and a leather vest which boldly displays the words *Savage Angels MC* across the back with a large sword-wielding angel. It's warm, so he's not wearing a shirt and has a lean, wiry frame with his six-pack abs on full display. He cuts a different figure than the hulking, solidly built Dane.

"*My* girl is fine. Just an early-morning craving."

He laughs. "Let me guess, apple pie?"

"Yeah, Judge." He scrubs a hand over his face. "I'll be glad when the babies arrive."

Howie comes out of the kitchen with a white box tied with string. "Dane, this is for Kat. If you give me a couple more minutes, I'll make you a breakfast burger to go."

Dane taps the counter. "Thank you, Howie. What would we do without you?"

The other man laughs. "Die of starvation."

"Good mornin', Judge. Do you want the regular?"

He gives Howie a thumbs-up, and I'm struck with how nice this is. They must all come here on the regular for Howie to know their orders.

"Ma'am?" I smile at Howie. "Do you know what you'd like?"

"My son will have the pancakes with a side of bacon."

"Nothing for you?"

"No, I'm good."

"Mom?"

Smiling, I say, "I'm fine, honey."

Zachary cocks his little head to the side, but he doesn't argue. When I look back at Howie, the other two men appear concerned.

"I'm not really a breakfast person. The coffee is

good and hot, so thank you for that."

Dane drinks his coffee, and Howie pours his friend one.

"Where's your new waitress?" asks Dane, and I'm grateful he changed the subject.

Howie shrugs and shakes his head. "Your guess is as good as mine."

Hearing this, I stand, and all three men stare at me.

"Um, I..." Words fail me under their scrutiny. "Well, it's just that—"

"Mom's a really good waitress. The best," Zachary states. "If you're willing to give her a chance, you can pay her today by giving us both breakfast. You won't regret it."

"Is that so?" asks Howie as he crosses his arms over his chest.

"H-he's right, I am." I smile awkwardly. "If you're not happy with me, I'll pay for our breakfasts."

Howie tilts his head to the side. "Sounds fair. I pay minimum wage, but you get to keep your tips. What would you like to eat?"

"Same as my son." Howie holds out his hand to me, and I quickly move to shake it. "Thank you. You won't regret it."

Howie smiles. "It's going to be a busy day." He leans over the counter, checking out my shoes. "Good, you've got sensible shoes on. The new girl wore heels. I told her not to but... vanity over common sense."

"I've waitressed before. This won't be my first rodeo." Letting go of his hand, I put my hand on my chest. "I'm Thea, and my son's name is Zachary."

"Howie, chief cook, part-time waitress, and owner." He points at the man who came in first. "This is Dane and Judge… they're regulars."

Dane gives me a subtle nod while Judge assesses me with a quick once-over.

"Hey, sugar, welcome to Tourmaline." Judge winks at me. "You single?"

Dane stands and shakes his head. "Ignore Judge. He's only playing with you." He looks at Howie. "I need to call into the clubhouse. Could you give my breakfast to Judge, and he can walk it down for me?"

"I will?" Dane remains silent and instead exchanges a glance with Judge, who takes a step back and offers a sign of agreement by holding up a hand. "I will."

Dane gives him a tight-lipped smile and me another chin lift and leaves.

"Is he your boss?"

"Worse. He's my president."

Howie belts out a laugh. "Be nice while I fix everyone something to eat." His eyes flick to me. "You'll be all right handling things while I cook?"

"Of course."

Howie smiles and goes into the kitchen.

Zachary tugs at my hand. "You okay, Mom?"

"Thanks for the save."

"Yeah, you had that deer-in-the-headlights look on your face."

Judge barks out a laugh, and I glance at him. "He's right, you did. Howie is good people. He'll do right by you if you do right by him."

"Thanks, and I will."

"You came in on the bus?"

"Yes."

"No one met you?"

"It was an unplanned trip, and he doesn't know we're here."

"Who are you looking for? I might know them."

"Renny Bennett."

Judge's smile fades, and he shifts his gaze between Zachary and me. "He a friend of yours?"

"Do you know Renny?"

"Sure do. He works in the garage at the end of town. I'm headed there as soon as Howie cooks breakfast. Do you want me to pass on the message that you're searching for him?"

"No!" I say a little too loudly. "I thought you were going to a clubhouse?"

"Yeah, I am. It's all in the same compound. Renny works as a mechanic for the Savage Angels."

"The MC?"

"Yeah."

My insides turn to liquid. I was hoping Renny

had changed, but here he is back in with the criminal element. And here I am with little to no money and nowhere to run.

"Are you okay?" Sitting back down, I nod. "You look a little pale."

Forcing a smile, I shake my head. "Just hungry. It's been a long few days."

"Where'd you come in from, sugar?"

The smile has returned to his face, but I have a feeling Judge is weighing up everything I'm telling him. If he is a friend of Renny's, I need him to know I'm not here to cause him any harm.

"Renny came to visit me a week ago. Told me he was living here with his sister, Destiny. Renny and I are old friends from before he went to prison."

"He went to prison?" asks Zachary.

"Yes, honey, but he didn't do it."

"How do you know?"

"I've known Renny Bennett since I was fourteen years old. He might be a little rough around the edges, but he's a good man."

Zachary's lips turn down at the sides. "He was the man we met on the way to the park?"

"Sure was."

"I liked him better than your other old friend."

Not wanting Zachary to tell Judge all our secrets, I laugh. "Me too. And thank you for helping me get a job. You did good."

His whole face lights up in a smile. "You're

not mad?"

"Why would I be mad? You helped me, little man."

Zachary grins. "And now we *both* get breakfast."

"We sure do."

Howie comes back out with a brown paper bag for Judge. "Here you go."

Judge pulls out his wallet and drops a couple of bills on the counter. "Thanks, Howie." He turns to leave but stops near the front door and locks eyes with me. "You have a good day, sugar."

Howie comes out from behind the counter and puts down our plates of food. "You sure you're going to be able to work today?"

"Absolutely, so long as you don't mind Zachary being here."

Howie grins. "Not at all. He can stay in the room out back, or there's an area behind the café. I've got a table and a couple of chairs out there. You won't be bored?" he asks Zachary.

"No, sir. Maybe I could help in the kitchen too? I'm good with dishes."

"Is that a fact? Tell you what, if you could rinse all the plates as I stack them, it'd be a huge help." Zachary moves his head up and down enthusiastically as he shovels a chunk of pancake into his mouth. "All right then, I'll leave you two to eat, and then we can get started."

For such a small town, Betty's Café has been bustling with activity all day. I quickly realized this cozy café is the hub for locals to trade gossip and catch up on the latest news. There's been a steady stream of what I'm sure are familiar faces flowing through the front door since it opened.

Now it's nearly three o'clock, and despite Howie forcing me to take a short lunch break at noon, exhaustion is setting in after three long days on the road with little sleep.

Howie is a friendly young man who has worked here his entire life before buying the café when the previous owner wanted to retire. The only real struggle he seems to have is finding reliable staff. It's easy enough in the winter when tourists swell the town's population, but when visitor numbers dwindle in the summertime, no one wants to work indoors on sunny days.

"You look beat."

Glancing up, Renny is standing in front of me. "Renny?"

"You seem tired, Thea. Why are you here?"

Wiping my hands on the apron Howie gave me, I say loudly, "Howie, can I take a break?"

"Sure. Take as long as you like. Zachary and I have it covered, don't we?"

"Sure do!"

Zachary has done more than simply rinse dishes—he's taken orders, refilled coffee cups, and tried his best to say hello to every customer as they walked through the doors.

"Follow me."

I lead Renny through the kitchen and out to the small courtyard tucked behind the café. The space is bathed in warm sunlight, the pale stones underfoot dotted with thriving potted plants. I settle into a metal chair at the lone table in the center, resting my elbows on its cool surface.

Renny steps outside, his observant eyes scanning the area and possible exits before joining me at the table. He sits across from me, his tall frame casting a shadow over the table's worn surface. Despite the sunny tranquility of the courtyard, there's an undercurrent of tension between us.

"I didn't even know this was here."

"I think it's Howie's secret. Did you know he lives upstairs?"

"No, but it makes sense. He's always here."

In the sunlight, Renny's eyes almost appear whiskey-colored. When he's angry, they used to take on a darker hue, but when he's happy, they resemble their current shade. He's wearing dark-colored jeans and a tight-fitting black T-shirt, accentuating his broad shoulders and showing off his tattoos. My stomach dips as he rubs his chin and leans forward, his eyes searching mine.

"Why are you here, Thea?"

There's an edge to his voice, a hardness, meaning he isn't happy to see me. Swallowing hard, I try to smile, and Renny frowns at me. Shaking my head to calm myself, I take a deep breath and let it out slowly. I don't want to mess this up.

"Zachary is yours."

A crease forms between his brows, and he leans back. "And?"

"And?" I whisper.

Renny stands. "What do you want me to do with that?" He throws one arm in the air and then points at me. "You sent me to prison, Thea. *You*. Do you think by telling me we have a child together, I'm going to forgive you?"

The air rushes out of me as though he's slapped me. I should have realized Renny wouldn't care. Tears prick the backs of my eyelids as I quickly stand and walk back toward the café, but he grabs my arm and spins me around.

The tears spill down my cheeks, and I brush them away.

"Why are you crying?"

"I'm not."

Renny releases me. "Why are you here?"

"Zachary is the only good thing I've done in my life," I blurt out. My eyes are glued to his chest as I'm unable to bear the condemnation in his eyes. "I'd do anything to protect him. The people who put you in jail threatened him... and me." For a moment, I muster the courage to meet his gaze but quickly avert it. "I'm not asking for me. I'll go and leave him here. But I can't, *I won't* have Zachary hurt. If you ever cared for me, Renny, please take care of our son. I'm begging you."

CHAPTER 6

RENNY

Her tears strike at my heart, and hearing her beg to look after our son chips away at the vengeance that has permeated my soul. Shaking my head, I release her and step back. The moment I laid eyes on Zachary, I knew he was mine, but hearing Thea confirm it leeches away some of my anger toward her.

"Why didn't you tell me you were pregnant?" I ask in a softer tone.

Her hands go to the sides of her face, and her gaze hits the floor. "You were right. It was my fault you ended up in prison." Her lips go into a hard line, the struggle evident as she fights more tears that threaten to fall. "I messed up everything."

Cocking my head to the side, I study the woman I once loved, and I realize I *want* to forgive her. I want to believe everything and anything she tells me, but how can I? Her betrayal cost me eight years and a son I didn't know existed.

"You can stay. You can *both* stay."

Thea releases a shaky breath and meets my eyes. "Thank you, Renny."

Relief washes over her, and I watch the tension leave her shoulders.

Thea wraps her arms around herself and says, "What now?"

"Jackson MacKenzie, Steve Plant, Hunter Johns, Samuel Perth, and Derrick Long," I recite the names of the men who wronged me, and Thea's eyes widen. "Are they the ones after you?"

"Y-yes. Hunter always finds me, and no matter where I move, he eventually tracks me down. The others visit from time to time, but it's usually Hunter."

"He always wanted to be in charge."

"What now?"

"We need to find you a place to stay."

"I can't stay with you?"

Shaking my head, I say, "No. I'm living with Destiny and her fiancé, Kade. Give me an hour, and I'll sort out something."

"Thank you."

Bending to stare into her eyes, I say, "Tonight, you and I are going to sit, and you're going to tell me everything. Do you understand?"

"Yes."

I point at her to further prove my point. "No lies, Thea. You lie to me, and I'll put you on the first bus out of town."

She swallows and nods. "Okay."

"Judge said Howie gave you a job?"

"Yes, he's very nice."

"Don't fuck it up. Howie is good people, and he's respected in this town. He has a lot of friends."

Thea frowns. "I wasn't going to. I'm a hard worker and honest."

Without meaning to, I huff out a laugh. "Yeah, sure you are."

Her face crumples, and more tears fall down her cheeks. Not wanting to cause Thea more pain, I walk past her, through the restaurant, and out onto the sidewalk. Destiny is waiting there, peering through the café's windows.

"Is she here?"

"Yeah, Thea and *my son* are here."

"Did she admit it?"

"Yes."

"Well, that's good. I'll start the process of getting you visitation. I'm thinking one week on, one week off. How does that sound?"

My little sister has turned into one hell of a lawyer, but not everything needs to be worked out in a court of law. Some things are better dealt with in a less formal way. Vengeance being one of them.

“Thea and Zachary need a place to stay.”

“There’s the motel in town?”

“No. She and the kid are in danger. They need to be closer to home. I know I don’t have the right to ask, but...”

Destiny reaches out and grabs my hand. “What do you need, brother?”

“Can they have my room, and I’ll ask Dane if he has a spare room in the clubhouse?”

“You want that bitch to stay with me?”

“You and Kade are the only ones I trust to keep them safe. It’s all about Zachary, not Thea. For the time being, they are a package deal.”

Destiny chews on her bottom lip, and a slow smile stretches across her face. “I’ll kill her with kindness.”

Squeezing her hand, I grin. “Thank you.”

“I’ll be nice, I promise. Besides, I get to know my nephew.”

“Yeah, but here’s the thing… I don’t know if he knows who we are.”

Destiny’s hands go into fists, and she plants them on her hips. “Are you kidding me?”

“For the past eight years, it’s only been the two of them. Let Thea tell him. He seems like a good kid.”

Her eyes squint at me. “Fine. But she better tell him soon. I’ve got years of presents to make up for.”

Chuckling, I let her hand go. “Yeah, me too.”

The clubhouse is less than a ten-minute walk from the café, nestled in the industrial section at the far end of Main Street. The entire compound is fenced in by a six-foot chain-link fence, sealing it off from the outside world.

Inside the fence, the lot is dominated by two large buildings—the clubhouse on one side and the garage workshop on the other. This is where the Savage Angels work on repairs for anything mechanical.

Since getting out of prison, the men of the MC have gone out of their way to make me feel welcomed into the fold. Despite the foreboding exterior, the atmosphere within the compound feels more familial than dangerous. Still, the fence serves as a clear divide between the club and the rest of the sleepy little town.

Judge sees me coming and saunters over. "Did everything go okay?"

"Yeah, thanks for the heads-up."

Judge folds his arms over his chest. He's the joker in the MC, always poking the bear, which is Dane. But Dane trusts Judge with his wife, Kat, so although he plays at being a fool, I know he's not.

"She's in trouble, isn't she?"

"Yeah. The men who put me in prison keep tabs on her."

His lips turn down. "The boy, he's yours?"

"Yeah."

"She didn't tell you?"

Running a hand down my face, the scruff on my jaw scratching my palm, I try to explain my relationship with Thea.

"She's the reason I ended up in prison. I don't know all the details, but she *is* going to tell me."

Judge's eyes widen. "You sure the boy's yours then?"

"Yeah, I'm sure."

Judge reaches out and puts a hand on my shoulder. "You need anything... all you gotta do is ask. But some advice, Renny? Don't trust her. *Fool me once, shame on you, fool me twice—*"

"Yeah, I know, *shame on me.*"

His hand falls away, and he shakes his head. "No, brother. Fool me twice, and you'll find yourself in an early grave. I'll gladly dig the hole myself."

He turns and strides away with a chilling promise lingering in the air. I'm left reassessing my impression of the man. Behind the jokes and laughs, Judge clearly has a ruthless, dangerous side. The casual talk of digging graves makes it clear he's not to be messed with. His cheery exterior masks the hardened interior needed to do what must be done in the MC life. I make a mental note not to underestimate him again.

Walking into the clubhouse, Jonas, VP of the Savage Angels, is behind the bar, grinning at Rebel standing in front of him.

"Come on, Jonas, be a friend."

"No. You should have put in the request, and you didn't."

"Ruby is going to be pissed."

"And she should be. It's not like your anniversary just happened. You've had a year to plan it and let me guess, you've already asked all the guys to fill in for you, and they've all said no? I've got plans on Friday night with Addy."

"You and Addy have been together forever... she'll understand."

Jonas possesses a tan that gives his pale green eyes an almost otherworldly appearance. Judging by the intensity of his gaze fixed on Rebel, I wouldn't be surprised if the man burst into flames.

"The reason Addy and I are still together is because I don't fuck up dates. Now go before I put you on the night shift or send you to Vegas permanently."

Rebel sucks in a breath, and I think he's about to argue some more, but Jonas holds up a hand and points to the clubhouse doors.

"Permanently," he repeats.

Rebel slams a hand on the bar top and stalks out

of the building.

Jonas turns his attention toward me and offers a smile. "Hey, Renny, how can I help you?"

"Trouble in paradise?"

Jonas waves a hand in the air dismissively. "Just Rebel being Rebel. I feel for the poor guy. He and Ruby have hit a rough patch, but at the end of the day, he should have organized to have the day off. He didn't, and now no one can cover." Jonas shrugs. "Drink?"

"No thanks. Is Dane around?"

"Nope. He's on Kat duty."

"Do I want to know?"

Jonas chuckles. "It means he's looking after the twins and his wife, who is the size of a house. I almost feel sorry for him."

"Almost?"

Jonas smirks. "He's had it too easy for too long. Kat can be a wild child, but pregnant, with swollen ankles and a bad attitude, she's a force of nature."

"Right." I belt out a laugh. "I was hoping to talk to him."

"What's your problem?"

"I was going to ask if there's a spare room here at the clubhouse?"

Jonas wipes the bar top down. "Sick of the love birds?"

Shaking my head, I say, "No, Kade and Destiny

have been great. A friend and her son have come to town, and I said they could have my room. You know they've been renovating the house, so it's kind of a mess."

"Say no more. We always keep two of the rooms empty for nomads. You can have one of those."

"Thanks so much. You can take rent out of my paycheck."

Jonas' nose crinkles up in distaste. "No need. You work hard, and because of you, we got extra business from the old guy you helped the other day."

Two days ago, I was walking to work when I came across an elderly man who was trying to change a tire on his car. He couldn't get the lug nuts to loosen. Hell, I don't know how he even got the tire out of the trunk—the man seemed as if a gust of wind could have knocked him over. It took me all of ten minutes to get the tire replaced and him on his way.

"Really?"

"Yeah, turns out he's the father of the man who owns the car dealership in Pearl County. He's been searching for someone to service his cars, and because of your kindness, we're in negotiations."

"The old guy was okay. A little wary of me, though."

"You're scary as fuck, man. I'd be wary of you too." Jonas walks out from behind the counter and down a hallway. "Follow me," he says over his shoulder.

I've never ventured this far into the clubhouse before. This is their second clubhouse—the first one burned down. It's two stories, with most of the living quarters upstairs. The walls are painted black, with pictures of different Harley Davidson models mounted on either side.

Jonas opens a door at the end of the hall and walks in. He stops in the middle of the room and looks around. "What do you think?"

It has a double bed, a chest of wooden drawers, with a television sitting on top. The walls are white and bare, but it's all spotless.

"Compared to prison, this is great."

Jonas nods. "Yeah." He points to a door, which I assume is a closet. "Through there, you'll find your own bathroom."

"Serious?" I move to open the door. The entire room is covered in white subway tiles. There's a shower, single vanity, and toilet. "This is nice. Hell, I might stay permanently. Kade and Destiny only have one functioning bathroom."

He laughs. "I don't know why they bought that old place. Kade has more money than all of us put together. He could have built her a palace."

"Ahh... she didn't want a palace but a falling-down train wreck of a home they could do up together and make it theirs." I use my finger to make quotation marks in the air.

"For a smart woman, your sister can be dumb."

"Have you seen what they've done?"

"Only on the outside. I know they got a new roof."

"They have a long way to go, but it's amazing. They've tried to keep the original features of the home. They redid the wooden floors in my room, replaced the French doors, replastered the walls, rewired, and painted it. It looks good. You should come over and see for yourself."

Jonas tilts his head to the side. "Kade keeps saying when it's done, he'll have us over." He casts another glance around the room. "You good here?"

"Yes, and thanks, I appreciate it."

"All good. Fresh towels under the sink, and there should be fresh sheets in there." Jonas points at the chest of drawers. "You need anything, you know where to find me."

I sit on the edge of the bed and take in my surroundings. This room is bigger than my prison cell. The window above the bed lets in a lot of natural light, but I can't help feeling like I'm closed in. My transition from prison to my room at Destiny and Kade's was easy. Their house has two stories, and my room is at the front, on the far right. It has two French doors which open onto a porch. Sure, I couldn't walk onto the porch as I would fall through it, but I didn't feel penned in with both sets of doors open. Here, I feel like the walls are closing in on me.

There's a full-length mirror on the back of the bathroom door. My reflection stares back at me, and I remind myself I'm free. Nothing can put me back behind bars except my own bad decisions.

Tonight, I'm going to get Thea to tell me why she did what she did.

Will I ever trust her?

It's been eight years, yet the memories are still vivid—walking into a room full of blood and bodies as if it were yesterday—sent there by Thea's betrayal. I rub my chest at the dull ache that always seems to hurt when I recall the fateful night. I had eight years to plot revenge on her and the others. The memories of Thea haunt and stall any plans, the ache a constant reminder of the scars left behind.

There was a small group of us involved in stealing cars and reselling them. I'm good with anything mechanical, including breaking into cars and hot-wiring them. We were all working toward a common goal to raise enough money to open our own garage, where we did up older cars and sold them for a profit. All we needed was the money to help with the down payment.

One night, I stole a car from a finance guy. It was a 1968 Ford GT in mint condition. Stealing it was easy. It's what I found on the back seat that made me return it. He had left a briefcase, and the plans to ship three million dollars in laundered drug money were inside.

Clean drug money.

It was like taking candy from a baby.

With my crew, we went to a wharf in a shady area of town. It was common knowledge in the seedy underworld that the Juarez Cartel ran their shady business deals out of there. The hardest part was keeping out of sight and creating a diversion. Hunter, Steve, and I went after the money. Thea, Samuel, and Derrick created the diversion.

They stole a car, set it on fire and, with a pipe to steer it and a brick on the gas, sent it hurtling through the main gates at the entry to the wharf. People ran from the fiery diversion, giving us three the relatively easy task of locating the cargo container. It was painted a burnt orange, like all of the others, but the one we needed had the number 1515 painted in the top left-hand corner. Using bolt cutters, we cut through the padlock.

The inside of the container smelled like death. I remember retching as we entered. The money was behind a fake wall in three bags. Each bag weighed about one hundred pounds. We slipped the handles of the bags over our shoulders as though they were backpacks, closed the door to the container, and double-timed it out of the area.

No one knew who did it, and no one ever came looking for us. Three million dollars should have been split evenly between us. Unfortunately, the others got greedy, and I ended up being framed for murder, but none of them expected to be left out in the cold without a dollar bill between them.

They should have waited for me to hand over the cash, but they thought they knew where it was hidden. They were wrong. After we stole the money, we put it in the trunk of my car. For safety reasons, we were in three separate vehicles in case someone saw us. Each of us drove in different directions. Instead of following the plan, I took the money to an abandoned warehouse on the outskirts of town. One of the walls had a hidden compartment behind a panel. Not easy to spot, and unless you knew where it was, you'd never find it. Of course, I had no way of knowing if the warehouse would be there in eight years, but then I never thought I'd be going to prison. Thankfully, the warehouse is still standing, albeit a little more rundown.

If it weren't for Destiny pushing hard on the DNA evidence, time of death, and the eyewitness account of an elderly woman, I'd still be in jail.

Justice is coming for those who betrayed me, and I won't even have to lift a finger.

Thea is the only wrench in my plan. I was going to throw her to the wolves too, but she's my son's mother. And if I'm honest with myself, seeing her brings up old feelings and good memories.

As I reflect on the past, I thought we were happy.

Life wasn't easy. I was taking care of Destiny, working on the fringes of the law, but with our payday, it would have been better.

Thea only needed to trust me.

Instead, she turned on me.

Now, here I am, all those years later, reunited with my sister, free and getting a payday for wrongful imprisonment. The three million is still where I left it, but it's not something I want anymore. It was for a future I no longer have.

Reaching into my pocket, I pull out a small, worn velvet pouch. I loosen the drawstring and gently shake out the ring nestled inside. It's a vintage beauty—an ornate silver band etched with delicate scrollwork flanking the main stone. The center ruby is a perfect polished oval, its deep crimson facets twinkling in the light. The scrollwork swirls and spirals down the sides of the band, little tendrils of silver embracing the gemstone. I remember how carefully I hunted for this ring, picturing it on Thea's slender finger. I was waiting for the right time to give it to her, but now it remains hidden away, a symbol of unsaid words and unfulfilled promises.

Standing, I tuck the ring back in its pouch and put it back in my pocket.

Surveying the clubhouse room once again, I wish it wasn't so closed in, but I guess I'll have to get used to it.

CHAPTER 7

DANE

Kat is asleep upstairs, and the twins, Jesse and Kristen, are playing on the back porch. I'm grateful my wife is resting. This pregnancy is hard on her—morning sickness that won't quit and carrying twins is tough. The last time she was pregnant, her body swelled, shoes didn't fit, and it was difficult losing the weight, but this time, she's bigger, and I worry about her mental health. It's one thing for me to tell her she's the most beautiful woman on the planet, but another for her to look in the mirror and see how much her body has changed.

My phone rings, and it's Jonas.

"Hey, man, what's up?"

"Nothing, Prez, everything is running smoothly. Just wanted to tell you Renny is staying in one of our spare rooms here at the clubhouse."

"Is he joining us?"

"No. He's giving up his room at Kade's for a friend and needed a place to stay."

Looking out on the porch, Jesse pushes his sister, and I tap on the glass. His attention quickly shifts to me, and he appears embarrassed at being caught. He glances back at his sister, rolls his eyes, then holds out a hand to her. Kristen puts her hands on her hips and leans forward. I can't hear the conversation, but whatever it is, she's not happy. Jesse looks back at me and shrugs.

"Jonas, give me a second." I open the sliding door. "Play nice."

"He started it!"

"I did not!"

"Enough, or I'll finish it."

The fire goes out in Kristen, and her hands drop to her sides. "Yes, Daddy."

Jesse's lips twist into a grimace, and he says, "Yes, sir."

I close the door, but not before I see Kristen lean in and say something to her brother, who then throws his arms up in the air and walks to the other end of the porch to get away from her. It's my fault. I spoil both of them, but Kristen is my princess.

"You there, Jonas?"

"Yeah, Dane... everything okay?"

"Kids," I state by way of an explanation. "I don't think it's such a good idea for Renny to be at the clubhouse."

"You want him to join us before we let him?"

"No, that's not what I meant. The rooms downstairs are small with tiny windows, and the guy just spent time in jail. It's not a good fit."

"You worried he'll go postal?"

With a laugh, I settle into a chair at the dining room table, phone in hand. "Something like that." I have cabins for rent on my property. It's the off-season, with only one couple staying here, so there's plenty of room. "Do you think he'd want to stay out here for a bit? I could put him up in one of the empty cabins, or his friend could take it." The low season makes for a peaceful retreat, exactly what Renny might need right now.

"I could ask?"

Wanting to get out of the house, I shake my head and say, "I'll do it. I'm going stir-crazy being here."

"Thought you were working on a basket case?"

A basket case is a bike we put together using old parts. If they're nice enough, we sell them.

"The noise bothers Kat, and she's asleep right now. And the twins look like they're ready to kill each other. A drive into town might be something we all need."

Jonas chuckles. "Want me to ask him to wait for you?"

"Yeah. I'll come right in."

Ending the call, I stand and open the sliding door.

"Who wants ice cream?"

Kristen immediately smiles at me and comes running. "Me!"

Jesse, who Kat calls her little old man, shakes his head at her and walks toward me slowly.

"You don't want ice cream?"

"I do, Dad."

Putting a hand on his shoulder, I look at Kristen. "Go get in the car. We'll be a minute."

Kristen smirks at her brother and runs from the room.

"Want to talk about it?"

"Why does she have to be so annoying?"

Smothering a laugh with my hand, I pluck the keys off the holder near the refrigerator. "Don't let her get under your skin. Your sister loves you, but she's missing her mom."

"Doesn't feel like she loves me. And you always take her side, Dad."

With a hand on his shoulder, I herd him toward the front door. "I know it seems like that, but I don't."

Jesse doesn't say anything as we climb into the car.

"Did you get in trouble?" asks Kristen in a sing-song voice.

Twisting to stare at her, I shake my head. "No, he didn't. You, young lady, be nicer to your brother."

Her face falls, and her bottom lip immediately

trembles. Taking care of my children is harder than running an MC. At least when I growl at my men, no one cries. Jesse has a soft heart, and although his sister annoys him, I watch as he moves closer to her and puts his hand in hers. She sniffles and shuffles closer to him. Being twins, they share a bond, and like I knew he would, he comforts her for my stern tone.

The trip into town doesn't take long. When I park the car, I turn to look at my children. "This is a quick visit, and then we'll go visit Howie at the café. Mind the rules for being in the clubhouse." Jesse nods as does Kristen, but she avoids eye contact with me. "Okay, everybody out."

Kristen opens her door, and Jesse goes out through it too. Being a father is one of my greatest joys. My children fill me with pride, but it's also one of the hardest jobs I've ever done. No one tells you how manipulating a child can be. Thankfully, Kat and I are almost always on the same page.

Taking the stairs two at a time, the kids run ahead straight to the pool tables at the back of the clubhouse.

Jonas is behind the bar, and Renny is sitting on a stool waiting for me.

"If you don't want me to stay, Dane, I can rent a room at the motel in town."

Smiling, I shake my head. "It's not that. Walk with me to the garage?" I don't wait for him to answer. "Jonas, will you keep an eye on those two?"

Jonas walks around the bar toward my children while Renny falls into step beside me.

"Have you thought about becoming a prospect?"

"Yes. There are a couple of things I need to do first."

Nodding, I keep walking until we come to the door of the garage office. "The rooms downstairs aren't made for living in long-term. I'm not sure if you know this, but out at my home, I have cabins I rent out to tourists. Anyway, it's not busy right now, and I thought you or your friend might feel more comfortable out there."

"Did Judge tell you who she is?"

With a quick shake of my head, I say, "No." Searching for the right words, I cross my arms across my chest. "A woman? Makes no difference to me. The cabins are light and airy. They've got kitchenettes, a bathroom, and a king-size bed. It's yours if you want it."

"How much?"

"No charge."

Renny frowns, his lips turning down. "Wouldn't be right."

"They aren't booked. If it were winter, you'd be shit out of luck. This isn't charity but me offering you an alternative to a one-window room in a clubhouse full of testosterone."

"I'm used to being in a confined space with men

trying to prove their dominance."

"Yeah, you are. But here's the thing... you're free now and should have all the space you need."

Renny studies me for a moment. "Thank you."

Reaching into my pocket, I pull out my wallet and hand him a business card. "My address is on there. Come to the main house, and I'll show you around."

"Thanks, Dane. I owe you."

"Yeah, you do, and one day, I'll call it in." Holding out my hand, Renny shakes it. "See you later."

Walking back toward the clubhouse, Renny calls after me, "Don't you need to call into the office?"

Looking over my shoulder, I say, "Nah, they've got it covered. I promised my kids ice cream."

CHAPTER 8

RENNY

Dane walks away, and in my gut, I know he understands me.

The thought of being cooped up in that room wasn't sitting well with me, and he somehow knew. The offer to stay in a cabin alone, without having to deal with people, is so much more appealing. I won't have to watch my back or sleep with one eye open, not that I think anyone in the MC would mess with me, but being in prison conditions, you expect the worst in men.

The way he offered me the cabin was even done so no one else could hear. I'm sure he probably ran it past Jonas, but he talked to me privately to put me at ease.

He's a good president, and something tells me when Dane calls in the favor I owe him, I'm not going to mind.

Looking at my watch, it's close to five o'clock. Swearing to myself, I jog back to Betty's Café. Thea isn't out the front when I enter, only Howie.

"Hey, man, is Thea here?"

Howie smiles. "She's out back with Zachary. Please go ahead." He flicks his head toward the back of the café.

Nodding at him, I walk through the building to the back door. Peering outside, I see Thea talking to Zachary. She's smiling at him, and my heart thuds in my chest a little quicker. He throws his arms around her, holding on tight. Pushing open the door, it creaks loudly, and the two turn to stare at me.

"Sorry for the wait," I say as I approach. "You two ready?"

Thea stands, her hand clasping Zachary's. "Renny, meet Zachary, your son. Zachary, this is your dad."

The boy's suspicious eyes, so like my own, stare back at me. "Mom told me you were in jail," he states bluntly.

"I was for a while, yes."

"She said you didn't do it."

"She's right, I didn't. Your mom knows the truth."

Zachary cocks his head, brows furrowed. "But they said you were guilty."

"They did, initially. But then they realized they

were wrong." I gesture toward the diner. "You two eat dinner yet?"

"No," Thea replies, gazing down at her son.

"Well, let's fix that. Howie's fried chicken may not beat your mom's, but it'll do the trick."

Thea's head swivels sharply at the mention of her cooking. "You remember my fried chicken?"

I give a slight nod before turning back inside, the memories clear as ever. There's little about Thea I've forgotten over the years.

When I return to the café, Dane sits inside, chatting with Howie while the kids watch with grins on their faces.

"Hey, Renny," Dane greets me. "Been a while."

"You only saw him at the clubhouse, Dad," his daughter interjects with a giggle.

Dane tilts his head playfully. "Did I now?"

"I saw you two talking," she insists, giggling again.

"Guess he's getting old," Howie jokes.

The girl's eyes widen as she laughs louder.

"All right, enough teasing if I'm getting you ice cream," Dane says. "You two decide what you want?"

His son pipes up, "Chocolate, please."

"Dad, can I get strawberry?" the girl asks.

"Of course."

Howie looks at Dane. "Anything for you or just coffee?"

"Coffee's fine. Thanks, Howie," Dane replies.

I move past them and sit in a booth by the window facing the door. Soon Thea emerges, her arm around Zachary.

"Hey, Thea, how was your day?" Dane asks.

To my surprise, he knows her name. Maybe it's jealousy or simply the fact he uses her name with such ease as though they are long-standing friends.

"Long but good," Thea replies. "Such nice people here."

Dane nods. "That we are." He glances my way before asking Thea, "Renny's your friend?"

Thea appears uneasy. "Yes, he's Zachary's father."

Dane's eyes widen. "Small world, huh?"

Ushering Zachary ahead, Thea says, "It sure is."

Zachary slides across the booth's seat to make room for his mom. This leaves Thea sitting opposite me. Shyly, she lowers her gaze, her attention on the menu.

"I bet you've got it memorized."

Thea puts it down and says, "I do." Not knowing what to do with her hands, she clasps them in front of her, then changes her mind and puts them under the table. "The fried chicken looks good."

Dane is walking his kids toward the exit when he stops by our table. "Have a good night, you three." Then only to me, he says, "I'm up late. Knock on the front door when you get to the house. Don't use the bell in case Kat's asleep."

"That's where I know you from," exclaims Thea. "You're Kat Saunders' husband."

Dane chuckles. "No, I'm Dane Reynolds, and Kat is my *wife*."

"I've been trying to figure out all day why you seemed so familiar. Your picture is always on her social media."

"You're a fan?"

"Honestly, who isn't? The Grinders are the band of my generation. I was devastated when I thought Kat was going to leave them. I'm so glad she didn't."

Dane grins. "It was a hard battle, but she made it. While you're in town, you should come out to the house with Renny and meet her. I'm sure she'd love it."

Thea's eyes bulge. "I-I'd love to."

Dane nods at me. "We'll set it up then, yeah?"

"Sounds good."

Thea claps her hands, and Zachary rolls his eyes at his mother's excitement.

"You all have a good night." Dane dips his chin and walks out of the café with his children running ahead of him.

"Oh my God! I'm going to meet Kat Saunders."

"Calm down, Mom."

"Do you know who she is?"

Zachary rolls his eyes. "She's in The Grinders."

Howie leans on the counter and says, "She's in

here all the time. Most of the band members come in from time to time. Did you three want anything to eat?"

"We'll have the fried chicken, please." I pick up the menu and study the sides. "And some fries, green beans, and mashed potatoes and gravy. Enough for three."

"Done deal." Howie walks out the back.

I can feel Zachary's eyes on me.

Putting my hands on the table, I look at him. "You can ask me anything, and I'll tell you the truth."

"Did you do it?"

"No."

"Did you love my mom?" Sucking in a breath, I nod once at him. "How come I didn't know you were my dad?"

Part of me wants to protect Thea, even though she doesn't deserve it. "I was in prison, and your mom had to take care of you all by herself. But I'm out now, so she told you."

Casting a glance at Thea, her face is red, and I'm not sure if it's from embarrassment or guilt. She gives me a small smile and places her arm around Zachary.

"We don't need to ask Renny everything right now. You can think about what you want to know."

"Like what?"

"Well, Renny has a sister. Her name is Destiny,

and she said we could stay with her for a little while."

"Is that true?" he asks, staring directly into my eyes.

"Yes. She's excited to meet you. In fact, she was stalking you earlier through the windows."

A smile spreads across his face. "I have an aunt? Do I have to call her that?"

Shaking my head, I say, "You can call her whatever you'd like... Aunty Destiny, Aunty, or even just Destiny. Whatever makes you feel more comfortable."

"What do I call you?"

Glancing between Zachary and Thea, I take a breath. I want to say Dad, but he's only just met me, and it wouldn't be right.

"For now, Renny. Later, if you want, you can call me Dad, but there's no pressure. It's all up to you."

Zachary nods. "Okay, Renny."

"How about you? Do you like being called Zachary?"

"My friends call me Zach, but Mom never does."

"Can I call you Zach?"

He grins. "Yeah."

The conversation flows smoothly, and I can tell by his manners and how he treats his mother that Thea has done a good job raising our son. Zach is a good kid.

The café fills up with customers, and Thea gets

up to help, leaving Zach and me to talk. I keep it simple. I ask about school, his mom, and what he likes to do in his downtime.

"I love baseball." His mouth turns down. "I'm pretty good at hitting but not so good at throwing."

"Practice makes perfect."

"You sound like my coach."

I chuckle. "Yeah?"

"Yeah. Are we going to live here now?"

His question takes me by surprise. "I don't know. That's between you and your mom."

"Would you like us to?"

Splaying my hands out on the tabletop, I give a deliberate, gradual approval. "Yes, but it's not so easy, Zach."

Zach looks at his mother serving customers and smiles. "She's running."

"What?"

"Mom wants me to think we're going back, but we've moved enough times that I know when she's running."

"Why do you think she's running?"

"Whenever someone from her past shows up, Mom moves on." He sighs. "This is the first time she's ever run *to* an old friend."

Zach sees things his mother might not want him to—he's pretty perceptive for a little kid.

"How many times have you moved?"

"Too many to count."

The men who put me in prison still haunt Thea. After all these years, what could they possibly think she would know or tell me?

Thea comes back to our table and stifles a yawn. "It's been a long day."

"How about I get you two settled at Destiny's?"

Thea nods. "Yes, please."

Turning, she waves at Howie, who comes out from behind the counter. "Thank you both for today. Are you available tomorrow?"

"Really?" Thea asks.

"You were a godsend today. The job's yours for as long as you need it." Howie casts me a quick glance.

"What time would you like me here?"

"I'll handle the morning rush, but if you could be here at ten, I'd appreciate it."

He holds out a brown paper bag. "Inside is some fried chicken, mashed potato, and a couple of slices of apple pie."

Tears form in Thea's eyes, and she wraps her arms around Howie's neck. Awkwardly, he pats her on the back then he looks at me, and I bark out a laugh.

"Come on, Thea, leave Howie alone."

Thea lets him go and stands back.

Howie's face has turned beet red. "See you tomorrow." He moves quickly back behind the counter and places her suitcase in front of her.

Walking outside, I put my hands in my pockets. "Destiny doesn't live far from here. Are you right to walk?"

"Sure, lead the way." Thea drags her suitcase behind her, the wheels jumping over the cracks in the pavement, so I bend to pick it up and carry it. Our hands brush against each other, and a spark of electricity jolts through me.

Thea flinches away from me. *Did she feel it too?*

"It's got wheels. I can do it."

"Woman, just let me help you."

Zach smiles, and the three of us walk along Main Street.

CHAPTER 9

THEA

Glancing up at Renny, his eyes are firmly planted on the sidewalk. He's carrying my suitcase as though it weighs nothing, his T-shirt taut across his chest.

Self-consciously, I smooth my dress and wish I wore something more flattering and not covered in food from the café. Not that Renny seemed to notice. Not that I blame him. Hell, Renny probably hates me.

With a sigh, I try to keep pace with Renny. Zachary is beside him, asking so many questions about the town and himself. Renny doesn't seem to mind. In fact, for someone who's been in prison for as long as he has, he's pretty damn good with a seven-year-old.

Destiny's house is on a tree-lined street. It's a two-story home painted white with black trim—it's picture-perfect for this little town. As we approach the front door, it swings open, revealing Destiny's smiling face. Her dark hair cascades over her shoulders, perfectly framing her large brown eyes. Though dressed in an oversized tee and yoga pants, she carries herself with an effortless grace that I've always secretly envied. I'm suddenly self-conscious in my travel-rumpled clothes. Destiny has always had a casual beauty about her, and it makes me wish I'd been blessed with her long limbs and feminine curves. But she greets me warmly, no hint of judgment in her eyes. Linking her arm through mine, she leads us inside.

When she bends, she locks eyes with Zachary. "I've been waiting to meet you. I'm your Aunty Destiny, and you are most welcome."

Zachary stares up at me, and I place a hand on his shoulder.

"Thank you so much, Destiny. We really appreciate you letting us stay."

The home has polished wood floors, but you can see they need renovating. There is plaster missing off some walls, and drop sheets cover some of the floor.

"It's a work in process, but Renny's room, your room, has been done, and the bathroom upstairs is finished. Just don't go out onto the porch. We haven't fixed it, and you'll probably fall through."

Walking ahead of us, she hurries up the staircase

in the foyer. Renny ushers Zachary to walk ahead of him and then looks at me.

"Are you okay?"

"Yes. Your sister is incredibly generous in letting us stay here."

"One thing about Destiny… she means well."

He locks eyes with me for a moment, then takes the stairs two at a time. To keep up with him, I practically have to jog up them. The upper floor has white walls and doors. The only color is the hall runner—a deep red with white stitching down the sides. Destiny is at the far end of the hallway, smiling and talking to Zachary.

Renny's room feels airy with its crisp white walls and furnishings in shades of blue. The linens appear as if they were plucked straight from a catalog, complete with a coordinated comforter and rug. Even the decorative touches feel carefully curated, from the books lining the shelves to the ocean print on the wall. Renny always loved the sea so no doubt she designed it with him in mind.

"Mom, there's only one bed," states Zachary.

"It's okay, honey. We can share. I promise to stay on my side of the bed.

Zachary stares at Destiny and says, "She steals the blankets."

Destiny giggles. "Good thing it's warm."

He grins at her, and I can tell Destiny has made him feel welcome. She moves past me and points at a door further down the hall.

"Second door on the right is the bathroom. I'll leave you to get settled." She glances at the brown paper bag. "Smells like food?"

"Yes, Howie gave it to us."

Destiny holds out a hand. "Give it to me, and I'll plate it up for you both."

"Thank you."

With a final smile, Destiny leaves us.

Renny puts my suitcase on the bed and places his hands on his hips. "I'll be downstairs. Come find me when you're ready."

"Thank you, Renny."

He smiles, and my heart skips a beat. It's only when he speaks I realize the smile wasn't meant for me but for Zachary.

"Anything for my son."

After we eat, it takes a little while for Zachary to settle and get him to bed. He wants so badly to spend time with Renny and Destiny.

When he's asleep, I shower and change, then make my way back downstairs. Hearing hushed voices at the back of the house, I follow them and find Renny, Destiny, and another man who must be her fiancé, Kade.

I clear my throat, and the conversation stops. "Ahh, hey." Pointing over my shoulder, I say, "He's finally down. Thank you all so much for letting us stay here. We won't be here long. Just long enough to catch my breath, then we'll be gone."

"What kind of life is that for Zach?" asks Renny.

"We've done it before." I look up at the ceiling. "He's a good kid... he'll adapt."

Kade blows out a breath. "Seems like you've got it all figured out, lady. But it's no way for a kid to grow up."

"Kade's right. Zach already knows when a *friend* from your past comes to visit..." he raises a brow, "... you run," replies Renny.

"H-he told you that?"

Renny sits on a stool at the kitchen island. It has a light purple laminated counter, and the cupboards are all wood, which has turned orange with age.

Renny's eyes flick to Kade and his sister. "Can you give us a minute?"

"Yep." Kade strides from the room.

Destiny stops near me. "You can stay as long as you need. I'm looking forward to getting to know you *both*." She casts Renny a brief glance over her shoulder and then leaves us alone.

"Come here, Thea. Sit. Tell me why."

Drawing in a deep breath, I sit next to Renny on a stool. There's so much to tell, and if I stare at him, I'll never get the words out of my mouth. Clasping my hands in front of me on the counter, I take a deep breath.

"You weren't supposed to go to jail."

Renny twists to face me, and I can feel his eyes boring into me. "Look at me, Thea."

"No. I won't ever get through this if I'm staring into your eyes and seeing the hurt that lives there."

Renny huffs out a noise, and I glance at him.

"Okay. Tell me."

Head bent, staring at my hands, I say, "The night you got arrested, well, that was the day I found out I was pregnant. I was so excited, and you were the first person I wanted to tell. But I went to your house, the one you shared with all the guys." I give a self-deprecating laugh. "If I could go back, I would have waited for you to call. You said you would, but I couldn't wait."

"I wasn't there."

"No. Hunter and Derrick were there. Hunter snatched the test from the doctor right out of my hands and started to laugh. At first, I thought he was happy for us, and then he waved it at Derrick and said, *'This is what we've been waiting for. Now, he's finished.'* At the time, I had no idea what he meant."

I spread my hands flat on the worn laminated surface. "He held a knife to my stomach, cut me a little… I still have the scar."

Renny has a sharp intake of breath, and I tilt my head to stare at him.

"They told me they wanted the money. Derrick said you were on the way to get it, and I should ring you and tell you to meet me at that house. I didn't know…" I pause and look back at my hands. "I *should* have known."

"It's why you told me to leave the money in the car."

"Yeah. But you were smarter than they thought. You didn't even bring the money. I found out later, after you'd been arrested, that you'd hidden it. Samuel came back to the house to cut me loose and told me you'd saved him. He laughed and said you sacrificed yourself for him. All of them got together and told me I needed to find out where the money is…" I shake my head, "… was. When Zachary was born, I tried to keep away from them. I've moved so many times, but they'd track me down. Always with a warning." I laugh bitterly as a tear runs down my face.

"Every one of them threatened Zachary. If I'd known where the money was, I would have told them in a heartbeat to protect him. Hell, I would have sacrificed myself to make sure he was safe." Turning quickly, I put my hands over his. "Saying I'm sorry sounds pathetic for everything you've been through, but I am. I am *so* sorry, Renny. You were the most important person in the world to me, and I betrayed you."

His eyes are fixed on my hands over his. "You did it to protect our son."

"Yes, but I also did it to protect myself. When Samuel told me you told him to run because the police were coming, I knew I'd done the wrong thing. You would never have betrayed any of us the way we deceived you."

His gaze meets mine, and one of his hands moves to the back of his head. Renny pulls me in, resting his forehead on mine. "You did what any good mother would do. You protected your child. I forgive you, Thea."

Forgiveness was the last thing I expected from Renny. Open hostility and hatred, yes. Sitting here, crying with him holding me close, I so wish I could turn back the clock to when it was only the two of us.

Renny leans back, his hands leaving me, and then he runs them down his jeans several times as though he's wiping away my touch. Overwhelmed, I turn back to the wall and clasp my hands in front of me.

"Why do they still haunt you? The old crew, why?"

"They want the money. But most of all, they don't want me telling you they set you up."

Renny's bitter laugh reverberates around the

room. "Did they really think I wouldn't figure it out? Not one of them visited me in prison. I was a little slow on the uptake, but it didn't take a genius to figure out it was you and them."

Flinching at his words, more tears fall down my cheeks. "It was Samuel who killed those people. He said it was an accident, but he always had a mean streak. You used to say he had a strange way of exercising his demons... well, I think he found a way. Samuel is cruel, mean, and likes to hurt people. Without you to keep him in line, he became the monster I always thought he was."

Renny's hand rubs my back. "Why did Steve go along with it? Were all of them in on it?"

Steve was Renny's closest friend. They went to school together, but he was always jealous of Renny.

"They planned it together, and with my help, they got away with it."

CHAPTER 10

RENNY

Thea's words hang in the air. But it's not her fault. If there's blame to be cast, it's all mine. I should never have put her in a position of danger. She was right about Samuel. He had a nasty streak, but he was younger than us, and I thought with age and all of us to guide him, he'd be okay. To think he butchered those people makes my skin crawl. During the trial, I had to listen to what was done to them in gory detail.

Two women and one man.

The man was killed instantly, but the two women were tortured and died slowly. He was a drug dealer, and the women were customers, although there was speculation they worked for him as prostitutes.

To think someone I trusted could do that to

another human being all for money is abhorrent. Worse still, I called them friends. After Thea, Steve's betrayal hurt the most. We had been friends for a long time.

The moment I was arrested and none of them came to see me, I knew. I've often wondered if they were ashamed of what they did, but hearing Thea tell me they have kept track of her all these years proves they never cared.

I'm ashamed I ever let any of them near her. Being in jail for so long gives you perspective. It would have taken longer, but I would have eventually opened the garage, and my life could have been so different.

Thea wipes her face with her hands, and I move into the kitchen, pluck the tissue box off a shelf, and put it in front of her.

"Thank you." She pulls out several from the box and wipes her eyes and nose. "I shouldn't be crying. You're the one who paid with years of your life for our mistake."

"Crying isn't my thing," I say with a smirk, but Thea isn't looking at my face.

"Renny, I understand I'm probably the last person you want to see, let alone have to stay at your sister's house, and if there'd been anyone else to turn to, I would have."

"This is my mess, Thea, not yours. I'm the one who brought those men into our lives. Although I thought we were like brothers. It never occurred to me they'd want to cut me out of the deal. I still don't understand why."

"They never wanted to open a garage."

Frowning, I shake my head. "It's all we talked about. We boosted cars and sold them to fund the project. It was our end goal."

Thea sniffles and peers up at me. "It was yours and my dream, not theirs. They wanted easy money, and it fell into your lap. They knew you would use it to open a garage and have every tool known to man in it, leaving very little left over for fun. Steve never wanted it, either. He told me so himself."

Sitting back on the stool, I huff out a laugh. "Jesus, I didn't know them at all."

"No. Neither of us did."

Thea stands. "I'm tired. Could we pick this up again tomorrow after my shift?"

"Yeah. Sleep well."

"You too."

I follow her to the bottom of the stairs, watch her walk up them, then open the front door where Kade is sitting on a chair outside.

"Do you believe her?"

"I do." I shrug, drawing both shoulders to my ears. "But I also want to believe her."

"Because of your son?"

"No, because she's Thea. My Thea."

Kade's nostrils flare. "Not yours, and remember, it was because of her you ended up where you did."

"I might have forgiven her, Kade, but I haven't forgotten."

"Good." He stands. "You and Destiny have one thing in common... you love easily."

I laugh. "Are you saying my sister can do better?"

"Absolutely. I thank the gods every day she chose me, and every day I choose her. There's nothing we wouldn't do for each other. Can you say the same about you and Thea?"

"It's not that simple. I put Thea in the situation of having to pick me or her unborn child. She made the right decision. Was it the right decision for me? Fuck, no, and I wish I'd been the kind of man back then who could have taken another path. The men I surrounded myself with, I thought they were my family, but they weren't."

"No, they weren't."

"Have you ever been betrayed, Kade?"

A sad smile creeps across his face. "Yes. Not by those I choose to call family but by blood. My brother, Francis, was a serial killer." His words hang in the air, and then he says, "The ones I call family now are Destiny, Zeke, Dane, Dirt, and you."

"Me?"

"Yeah. I know you'd cut off your own dick than hurt your sister. It makes you trustworthy. What would Thea do to protect you?" Kade doesn't wait for an answer. He walks back inside and shuts the door.

Dane's home is nestled on the side of a mountain. When I turn into his driveway, I gaze up at the beautiful house. It rises three stories high, with sweeping porches wrapping around each level. For an MC president, he sure has a nice home. Opening the door to the car I borrowed from Destiny, Dane walks out and waves a greeting as he jogs down the stairs.

"Did you find the place okay?"

"Yeah." I gesture to his home. "Seems like you've got a nice setup."

Dane grins. "Hard work and perseverance." He dangles a set of keys at me. "Come on, I'll show you where you're staying."

With my hands in my pockets, I match his pace as we follow a driveway further down the mountain.

"It's a bit of a hike. Tomorrow, you can park down here. Tonight, I need the exercise and to get out of the house."

"So, you're using me?" I joke.

Dane nods. "Yep. It's been a long day. Kat is pregnant, and everything seems to upset her. The kids are fighting over everything. Give me the MC any day."

Laughing, I say, "So how many of these cabins do you have?"

"We started with three, now there's six. Might do more, but not here. Kat owns the property next door. Her land is steeper than mine, so it's harder to build on. They built the main house on the only really flat surface."

"There's no room left here?"

Dane shakes his head. "There is, but I don't want any more people wandering around my home. We get a lot of couples, but then we get those who want to see an MC up close or those who want to see The Grinders."

"Ahh... fans."

"Yeah."

He stops in front of a building painted dark blue with white trim and opens the door. We walk through a small entryway, and he tosses the keys into a bowl on a side table next to the front door.

"Small sitting room here with a kitchenette, and through here..." Dane keeps walking through a door, "... is the only bedroom. It has views down the mountain."

The bedroom would have natural light from the French doors and windows during the day, which take up nearly an entire wall. White curtains frame them but can be pulled back to reveal what I am sure is a breathtaking mountain view. Just outside the doors, a wooden deck extends from the bedroom, creating a space to relax.

The bedroom has a minimalist style with neutral tones. On one side is an open ensuite bathroom with a clawfoot tub, glass-enclosed shower, and double vanities. The ensuite feels like a spa you'd find in some posh hotel. It all feels a little too nice for a man like me.

Taking in the luxurious surroundings, I let out a whistle. "Are you sure it's okay I stay here?"

"Like I said, slow season, and you won't feel hemmed in here."

Rocking back on my heels, I ask, "You know the feeling?"

"I spent time in a boys' facility when I was younger. Nothing compared to what you went through, but I remember feeling cooped up after I got out." He cocks his head to the side. "The Savage Angels helped me, and I'm hoping they can do the same for you."

Dane sees and understands much, but I'm unsure why he'd want me in his MC.

"I'm not sure I'm a good fit." The last thing I want is to get involved with an MC and end up back in prison.

"You are." He makes a clicking sound. "There's

milk, bread, and a few other things in the mini-fridge." Dane claps me on the back as he walks to the front door. "You're welcome to stay as long as you like."

"Until the busy season?"

Dane chuckles. "You got that right. We're fully booked." He steps outside. "Renny, talk to the guys. We're not the MC we once were. Most of our business is clean. If you don't want to be associated with some of our other endeavors, that's cool. I've got enough who will. Think about it. We take care of our own, and Judge vouched for you."

Frowning, I ask, "Why would he do that? He barely knows me."

"Surprised me too. Judge has done nothing like that before, and he's got a cousin in the MC. He wouldn't vouch for him, but he did you." Dane looks up at the night sky. "Night, Renny. You need anything, come up to the main house."

"Thanks, Dane."

He gives me a two-fingered salute and disappears into the night.

I close the door and walk back into the bedroom. The windows are open, and a slight breeze moves the curtains. Sitting on the bed, I reflect on the day. Kade and Destiny are suspicious of Thea, although they're glad to get to spend time with Zach. While I understand their fears, it was me who put Thea in with those sharks. I introduced her to them, so ultimately, it's my fault she did what she did. If I'd been a better man, she would never have even met them. I believe her when she says she had to do what she did. It's my guilt to bear, not hers.

CHAPTER 11

THEA

Destiny was more than happy to look after Zachary for the day. He was a little apprehensive, but the moment she mentioned video games and ice cream, he was in. Howie told me to start at ten, but I came in at nine with a good night's sleep and Zachary taken care of. To say Howie was relieved to see me was an understatement.

"Hey, Thea, take a break. Grab yourself a drink and go sit down."

"You haven't stopped," I counter.

"Yeah, but I'm used to it, and it's my business." Howie pushes his glasses up his nose and smiles. "Go sit outside in the sun. It's a beautiful day."

A couple of the customers smile at me as I pour myself a cup of coffee and head for the back door of the café. The sun feels good on my skin. Closing my eyes, I raise my face to the sky and enjoy being off my feet.

A short time later, the sound of someone walking toward me startles me. It's Renny, and he has two slices of apple pie in his hands.

"Howie said you had coffee, and I thought you might like pie to go with it."

Renny smiles, puts it in front of me, then sits opposite me.

"Thank you."

"How's day two of being a waitress going?"

"Well, it's only day two here. I've been a waitress for a really long time."

Renny nods and then uses his fork to slice into his pie. "Judge said Howie has the best pies."

"He told me he uses the same recipes as the previous owner. Her name was Betty. But I guess you know all that."

Renny tilts his head to the side and says, "No, I didn't. I'm still getting to know everyone. I've made friends at the MC and the garage. I'm a bit of a loner."

Sipping my coffee, I say, "You never used to be."

"People change."

Feeling a little stupid at my comment, I dip my head and dig into the apple pie. It's slightly warm with a lovely crumbly pastry and almost melts in your mouth.

A groan escapes my lips, and Renny stares at me curiously.

"I'm sorry." I laugh. "It's really good."

"Don't apologize."

He smiles at me, and for the first time, it reaches his eyes. It's nice to catch a glimpse of the old Renny. It's nice to know he's still in there.

"The tattoos, do they mean something?"

Renny straightens out an arm, examining it. "Some, yes. Sometimes, I simply appreciated the art."

"You had a couple before you went..."

"Yeah, I did. My second year in, my cellmate was a tattooist. He was a true artist." Renny looks up at the sky and then points at his neck. "This one was the hardest to do. Having someone press down while you're trying to breathe and not move or swallow, well, to say it took a level of trust is an understatement."

His neck tattoo is a striking tattoo portraying an angel. Its wings gracefully embrace the sides of his neck, their intricate feathers unfurling in intricate patterns. The angel's face is shrouded in darkness. I study it for a moment more before Renny drops his head and stares at me.

"It's beautiful."

Renny's face turns a little red. "Ahh… not sure I'd describe it that way."

I take another bite of my pie. "No, you wouldn't.

You'd say it's bad or tough or..." A giggle escapes me.

Renny points at me with his fork. "Now you're getting it."

We laugh, and then we sit in comfortable silence, eating. When I'm done, I stand, as does Renny.

"I should get back. Thanks for the pie."

"I called in to see Destiny and Zach. They seem to be having a good time."

"She promised him ice cream. I'm sure he'll do anything she asks."

Renny crosses his arms over his chest, raises his eyebrows, and says, "I was hoping we could get dinner together. Destiny said she's happy to keep Zach."

My stomach does a flip. "Just the two of us?"

His arms fall to his sides. "Yeah, I don't want Zach hearing us talk about the crew. I was hoping you could give me all the information on them that you know. While they're still out there, they are a threat to both of us."

Here I was thinking Renny wanted to be alone with me, but, of course, he wouldn't. He wants to know all he can about his old friends and has no interest in me at all.

Do I blame him? No.

But a part of me wishes he'd look at me like he used to.

Eight years, a son he didn't know he had, and my

betrayal are probably enough to deal with for him.

With my best fake smile, I nod. “It’s a date. What time?”

Renny stares down at me, his eyebrows coming together. “What time does your shift end?”

“Howie closes early on Wednesdays, so I’ll be finished at five.”

“I’ll pick you up.”

“See you then.” Reaching out, I squeeze his arm, pick up the plates and my cup, and walk back inside.

CHAPTER 12

RENNY

My arm burns where Thea touched me. Sparks seem to fly whenever I'm around her. She's not the same woman I left behind. There's still a softness to her, but now it has a protective layer. I guess bringing up a child on your own will do that.

I follow her through the restaurant, smile at Howie, and then head for the Savage Angels' compound.

When I arrive, Judge is leaning against the office door and gives me a wave as I walk toward him.

"What's got you smiling?" he asks.

"Nothing."

"Bullshit. Someone's put a smile on your dial."

"What are you, ten?"

Judge studies me and then says, "Thea. You're smiling over Thea."

Shaking my head, I ignore him and walk into the garage. It has three bays and a car up on lifts in each one.

"Did she tell you why?" Judge is right behind me.

"Why what?"

There's a group of guys working on the cars.

Zeke sticks his head out from underneath one and grins. "What fucking time do you call this? Are you running on Judge time now?"

"Fuck you, Zeke. I was here."

"But were you working? No, Judge, you were hanging around wasting time."

Laughing, I ignore them, continue on into the changing rooms, and open my locker. Inside is a pair of overalls I pull on over my clothes.

Judge follows me in and leans against one of the lockers. "I know you think I'm busting your balls. And, man, I know it's none of my business, but… *do you believe her*?"

"Why do you care?"

Judge's lips turn down at the sides. "I had a brother who got all turned around over a piece of ass. Ended up dead. I guess you remind me of him, and I don't want you to end up the same way."

His honest admission surprises me. "They held a knife to our unborn child, so she did what she had to do to save him and herself. Do I believe they did that? Yeah, I do. Do I believe she's sorry? Yep. But do I trust her one hundred percent? No. And maybe

I never will. But for our son, I have to try."

Judge draws in a deep breath. "And the fuckers who threatened her, what are you going to do about them?"

"They're all going to pay."

Judge smiles and then pushes off the lockers. "You need any help, you come find me."

I follow him back into the workshop, where Zeke throws a rag at him. "Are you going to do any work today?"

Judge laughs. "Nope, I'm on Kat duty. And later, I'm on Daddy duty."

Zeke's face goes deadpan as he stares at Judge. "You could have told me that in the beginning."

"Yeah, but it's fun letting you think you can bust my balls."

"Your kid or Kat's for Daddy duty?"

"Mine. Dane is taking care of the twins."

A wicked smile creeps across Zeke's face. "Have fun."

Judge narrows his gaze. "And what does that mean?"

"You'll find out." Zeke lets out a maniacal laugh and goes back to work.

Judge's hands go to his hips, and he shakes his head. "You're a mean fucker to get a little kid, *my* kid, to do your dirty work."

Zeke ignores him, and after a minute, Judge stalks out of the building, talking to himself and shaking his head.

"Did you do anything to his kid?"

Zeke belts out a laugh. "Nah, just fucking with him this time. If there's one thing on the planet Judge can't discipline, it's his son, Noah. Well, Noah and his old lady, Jasmin."

"I'm yet to meet her. What's she like?"

Zeke scratches the side of his head and shrugs. "Different to Kat. Where Kat goes out of her way to make you feel welcome, Jasmin kind of ignores you. She has this permanent I'm-bored look on her face." Zeke smiles. "Except when she's around the rest of The Grinders, then she's animated in a way she's not around everyone else."

"Still finding her footing?"

"Nah, she's been around us for a long time now. I'd say she's shy, but she's not. Jasmin is a weird one."

Zeke goes back to work, and I move to the next car bay. It's an old Honda which has seen better days.

With most of the grease scrubbed off my knuckles and wearing a clean set of clothes, I wait outside

Betty's for Thea to finish work. She emerges from the diner, chatting with a customer. Hair from her ponytail has come loose, framing her lovely face. She's still wearing her work apron, stained from the day's specials.

As she turns to say goodbye, her eyes meet mine. A smile spreads across her face, and her eyes crinkle at the corners. She touches the woman lightly on the arm before walking over to me. If I didn't know better, I would swear Thea is happy to see me waiting for her.

"Hey, Renny."

"You seem like you've had a good day."

"Everyone who's come into the café has been really nice." Thea stares back through the front window and waves at Howie. "I don't understand why Howie can't get a good waitress. He's a great boss, doesn't charge me for lunch, *and* lets me keep my tips."

"Sounds like you're fitting in here pretty well."

"I'm trying. But don't worry, it's temporary." Thea gives me a once-over. "You look good, and I must look terrible." Thea lets out a nervous laugh and smooths out her apron.

"You're perfectly fine. The apron adds an air of..." I falter to find the right words.

"Authenticity to a woman who works hard?"

I belt out a chuckle. "Yep."

Thea shrugs. "So, where are we going, and do I

have time to shower and change?"

"I'm staying out at Dane and Kat's place. They're letting me use one of their cabins. It's got a killer view, so I was thinking we'd get Chinese from Pearl County and have it overlooking the valley below."

"Can I quickly go home and clean up?"

"Yeah. I'm sure you want to see Zach too."

"I do."

Destiny lent me her car, it's a Ford F150. I open the door, and Thea climbs in. I jog around the front and get in the driver's side.

"Whose car is this?"

"Destiny's."

"Are you sure?"

Nodding, I start the car, put it in gear, and pull away from the curb. "Yeah. Why?"

"I guess I thought she'd have something more feminine."

Thea has a point. You'd definitely think this car belonged to a man. It's black with lots of chrome, tinted windows, and thirty-four-inch tires.

"There's more to Destiny than meets the eye. She might look like a princess, but she can get down in the mud with the boys any day of the week." I point at the steering wheel. "But she's still a girly girl at heart." The Ford logo in the middle of the steering wheel has gemstones surrounding it.

Thea giggles. "I like it."

"Yeah? I'm not so sure."

She laughs louder, and I grin at her. This feels like old times when we used to go cruising together.

As soon as I park the car in the driveway, Thea jumps out and hurries inside. "I'll be quick," she calls over her shoulder.

Zach comes out to meet me. "Mom's quick isn't *our* quick. She takes for*ever*."

"Women always do, bud." I climb out of the car and shut the door. "What did you do today?"

His face lights up. "Aunty Destiny took me to meet her boss, Rush, and then we went to The Cherry to see her old boss, Tobias. He's inside." Zach opens the screen door to the house for me. "And then the three of us went to Pearl County for ice cream. I got chocolate, and Aunty Destiny even got me a pint to bring home."

Walking into the house, Tobias is sitting on the couch. His hair is pulled back into a man bun, and he's chatting easily with Kade. He gives me a chin lift and stands, extending his hand for me to shake.

"It's really good to finally meet you, Renny, without a plate of glass between us." He is as tall as Dane Reynolds and as well built.

Grasping his hand in my own, I shake it. "Nice to meet you too," I reply automatically. "You know, apart from telling me you were Destiny's boss, you never told me what it was she did for you."

"She worked for me." He looks at Destiny. "*Before* she decided to go straight." Tobias winks at her. “There’s always a job for you at The Cherry if you ever want to come back.”

“She doesn’t,” Kade replies.

Tobias and Destiny exchange a private smile.

“Oh, stop teasing him, Tobias.”

“Who’s teasing? I’m dead serious.”

“What’s The Cherry?” I ask, feeling a little out of the loop.

“A strip club. The Savage Angels own a few. Until she left, Destiny was one of our best performers until...” Tobias shrugs, then stares at me. “Well, until she left.”

“You were a stripper?”

Destiny nods. “I was. It paid my way through law school.”

“And you knew she was a stripper?” I ask Kade.

“Yep, it’s how we met.”

“Is there a problem?” Tobias asks.

“I didn’t know.”

Destiny stands and waves a hand in the air. “It paid well, and unlike some clubs, I didn’t have to strip all the way down, and Tobias never made me sleep with any of the customers. The Cherry has a strict no-touching policy.” She smiles warmly at Tobias. “You were a great boss and are a very good friend.”

Tobias grins. “The offer is still there.”

“How come you never told me?” I look between Destiny and Tobias.

Destiny shrugs. "You're my brother, and I didn't want you worrying about me. Tobias takes care of all his girls, and the Savage Angels kept us safe."

Kade and Tobias exchange a glance.

Tobias clears his throat. "Time for me to go." He pulls Destiny into his arms for a quick hug, shakes Kade and Zach's hands, and turns to leave. "Renny, walk me out?"

"Sure."

Outside, parked in front of the house, is a red Dodge Challenger Demon. Renny walks to it and leans against it.

"D is happy you're back."

"I'm happy to be back."

He nods and tilts his head to the side. "I have a lot of friends."

"Yeah?"

"Yeah," he replies firmly. "One of my friends says you've been asking about Steve Plant."

"What's it to you?"

He points to the house. "I care about Destiny and Kade, and I don't want you bringing your shit down on them."

"Who says I'm going to?"

"Steve Plant isn't to be fucked with. His crew works and plays hard. If you're caught fucking with him, he'll burn your house down with everyone in it."

"His crew was *my* crew. They owe me, and I'm

going to collect."

"You knew him before you went away?"

"Yep. Not that it's any of your business, but Steve was my best friend, and he and his crew were the reason I went to prison. Like I said, he owes me."

Tobias sucks in a breath, his nostrils flaring slightly. "If you need intel, you come to me. Your sister is like family. I don't want to see her hurt." He opens the car, leans in, and holds out a card to me. "You need anything, you ring me. I can get things done quietly so it doesn't come back to haunt you or your sister."

The card has The Cherry printed on one side and a phone number on the other.

"Thanks."

Tobias holds my gaze, and his lips go into a thin, hard line. "I know you can handle yourself. There were stories about you in Glenford." He leans in a little closer. "But it's not only about you anymore." Tobias points at the house. "There are a whole lot of people in there who could get hurt if you try to go it alone."

Being out—it's hard to trust those around me.

In prison—I looked after myself.

But I know Tobias is right.

"I have a list. There's one person I can't find, and that's Steve."

"Do you have a plan?"

"Yes."

"Care to share?"

"No." I move to stand next to him and turn to face the house. "I don't know you anymore. Eight years ago, you were on the fringes of my world. I'd heard stories about you, and when you came to visit and said you were looking after Destiny, I was grateful. But I'm out now, get me the information I'm asking for, and after I've asked around, maybe I'll trust you."

"Your sister trusts me."

"Yeah, and she ended up stripping. Good job," I reply sarcastically.

Tobias laughs. "You don't fucking know her at all. Did she seem embarrassed telling you what she did? Did it look like she wanted to throw me out or have Kade beat me to a pulp? It was me who took care of her while you were gone. You'd best remember that."

Tobias gets in his car, and without a backward glance, I walk back to the house.

Destiny is waiting for me in the kitchen.

"Did he give you the big-brother speech?"

"More or less. Do you trust him?"

"I trust Tobias with my life."

Kade walks up behind her and wraps his arms around her waist. "Me too. He's a moody fucker, but he'd do anything for Destiny."

Thea enters the kitchen. Her hair is wet, and she

looks a little frazzled. "I'm ready."

"Good. Let's go."

"Wait!" Destiny breaks out of Kade's embrace. "Do you need anything washed for tomorrow?"

"Yes!" Thea does an about-face and runs back upstairs. I can hear her footfalls from one side of the house to the other.

"Can I come?" asks Zach.

"Not tonight, bud. There's a few things I need to talk to your mom about."

"About me?"

"Yes."

"You want us to go?" Zach has a crease between his brows.

"No. The opposite, but I know you have a life, school, and friends where you used to live. I guess I want to know what your mom wants to do."

"Do I get a say?"

"Yes, but only after I've talked to your mom."

Destiny puts an arm around him. "You and your mom are welcome to stay here as long as you need or want to."

Zach smiles up at her and puts an arm around her waist. "I like it here."

My heart swells at his admission.

Tonight, I want to talk to Thea about staying so I can get to know Zach better, but she has a life and presumably a job to go back to.

Hell, she might even have a boyfriend.

And that thought right there stops me in my tracks.

I still want and care about Thea.

Thea walks back into the room with an armful of clothes and hugs Zach. “Be good for Aunty Destiny and Uncle Kade. I’ll be back a little later.” She ruffles his hair, and he grins at her.

“Yes, ma’am.”

Thea locks eyes with Destiny. “No ice cream.”

“Mom!”

Thea laughs. “How much did you have today?”

His gaze drops to the floor, and he shrugs. “I’m not mad, honey.” He looks up at her. “I just want to make sure you have all your teeth when I get home.”

Zach giggles and nods. “Okay.”

He hugs her tightly, and Thea winks at Destiny. “Thank you for taking care of him.”

Destiny smiles. “He’s no trouble.” Destiny looks at me. “You said you were going to get Chinese from Pearl, so I got you your favorites.” She stops and waves a hand in the air. “Well, what used to be your…“ Destiny appears flustered. “I should have called.”

“It’s good, D. Thank you. Saves us a ride.” I pull her in for a quick hug, then lean back and smile down at her. “Tell me you got me egg rolls.”

With a huge grin, she says, “Yes, I did.”

Keeping an arm around Destiny’s shoulders, I

stare at Thea. “Are you ready to go?”

“Sure am.” She holds up her bundle of clothes. “Where would you like them?”

Destiny removes them from her arms. “I’ll take them.”

My sister seems to have thought of everything.

The way she’s accepted me and now Zach and Thea into her life amazes me.

The drive out to the cabin with Thea in the car is awkward. Neither of us speaks, and when I pull up in front of the building, Thea appears nervous.

“Hey, if you don’t want to talk, we can just eat, and I’ll take you back into town.”

“I’m so sorry. There are a million things I want to say, but I don’t know where to start. I’ve thought about this so many times.”

“About what?”

“About what I would say to you. How you would react.” She sighs and twists her hands in her lap. “But now you’re here, I don’t know what to say.”

“How about you come inside, we eat, and in between stuffing our faces, you tell me about your life.”

Thea huffs out a laugh. "I can do that."

We open our doors, and I lead the way into the cabin. The Chinese smells good. I put it on the bench in the kitchenette and open a cupboard to find bowls. Thea opens a drawer and pulls out spoons and forks. The tension between us feels as though it's subsided for now.

"Where are we eating?"

"Ahh… come with me."

The sun is low in the sky when I lead her through the bedroom and out to the deck. I put the Chinese and the bowls on a small table.

Turning, Thea is standing in the doorway, her hand to her chest. She's bathed in the last rays of the day, giving her an ethereal appearance.

"It's beautiful."

Staring at her, I say, "Yeah, it is."

She steps out onto the deck and sits in a chair. "Do you have anything to drink?"

"Damn. I knew I'd forget something. Water?"

She giggles. "Water is fine."

Walking back inside, I open the small bar refrigerator and pull out two bottles of water.

A knock sounds on the front door, and I open it.

"Hi! Sorry to bother you. I'm Kat, Dane's wife." She thrusts a bottle of wine at me. "He was supposed to put this in your mini bar, but he forgot." She tilts her head from side to side. "Sorry."

I take the wine out of her hands. "Ahh… you

know I'm not a paying guest?"

Kat chuckles. "I know. You're front-page news, I know about you, and Destiny is a friend."

"Renny, what's keeping you?" Thea asks as she walks toward us.

"Me! Sorry. I'm just dropping off a bottle of wine. I hope white is okay?"

"Oh my God! You're Katarina Saunders," shrieks Thea.

Kat holds out her hands in front of her. "Just Kat."

Thea pushes past me. "Kat? You said I can call you Kat?" Thea glances at me. "I can call her Kat."

Frowning, I push Thea slightly back. "Yep, I heard her. Kat, would you like to come in? We've got enough for a small army."

Kat stares back toward the main house. "Maybe for a minute?"

Thea stumbles backward as Kat moves through the cabin and out to the back deck. Thea's eyes are as big as saucers, and her mouth is open.

"Why don't you join Kat, and I'll get another bowl and fork for our guest."

Thea nods mechanically and does as I ask. I've never seen someone so starstruck. I grab the extra bowl and fork and a couple of wine glasses. When I get out there, Thea and Kat are talking like long-lost friends.

"I remember with my pregnancy with Zachary, I was sick for months. And coffee, the very smell of it was unbearable."

Kat waves a hand at her. "Tell me about it. But for me, it's the smell of beer. Dane kissed me the other night, and I nearly vomited in his mouth." Kat shivers and rubs her arms. "So not good."

I place the extra bowl between the two women, and Thea dishes out the food.

"Kat, would you like a glass of wine?"

Thea gazes at me with a look of disdain.

"No, I can't. I'm pregnant."

"I thought it was okay to have a glass?" I say, staring at Thea.

"No, no amount of alcohol is good for the baby."

"Babies," corrects Kat.

"You're having twins?"

Kat smiles. "My second set. I've already got Jesse and Kristen."

"I knew that. Well, congratulations!"

Feeling like a third wheel, I walk back inside and grab a chair from the small table in the kitchenette.

The two women are deep in conversation as I place the chair near them. Opening the bottle, I pour myself and Thea a glass of wine and pick up a bowl. Thea has divided up the food and put two egg rolls on top of mine. I eat the egg rolls first, and they taste as good as I remember.

"What about you? What brings you to Tourmaline?"

Thea picks up the wine glass and takes a sip. She

glances at me, then back at Kat. "Well, the truth is, ahh… well, I was Renny's girlfriend before he went to prison. My son, *our son*, Zachary, is Renny's, and they've never met." Thea gazes out at the fading view. "And we're in trouble, so I came here to ask Renny for help."

Kat reaches out and touches Thea. "You did the right thing. When trouble comes calling, there's nothing like family to help." Kat stands and nods at me. "Walk me out?"

"Sure."

"It was so nice meeting you, Thea."

"Please stay."

Kat shakes her head. "I have a family waiting on me, and it sounds like you two have a lot of catching up to do. We'll see each other again. I'm always in visiting Howie. He makes the *best* pie."

Kat steals an egg roll and heads for the front door. I follow her back through the cabin. Kat stops on the other side of the front door.

"Dane likes you, Renny."

"He does?"

"Yeah. So, because you're a man, and sometimes men can be dumb, I'm going to say this." She bites into the egg roll, chews it, and swallows. "If you need help with *anything*, you ask. Dane thinks you'll be a good fit for the Savage Angels, and he's a good judge of character." She smirks. "Hell, he married me, didn't he?" Kat pats me on the chest. "Don't be a stranger."

Kat walks away, eating her egg roll, and I'm left wondering what kind of town Tourmaline actually is? It's filled with small-town country people who all seem nice, but it's also got one of the most ruthless MCs inhabiting it.

One contradicts the other.

And I'm wondering when the two will collide and how it will end for me.

CHAPTER 13

THEA

Katarina Saunders, Kat, my idol, just sat and talked to me. Unfortunately, I think my confession as to why I'm here scared her off.

Renny comes back and sits in her chair.

"You're not hungry?"

Picking up my bowl, I use the fork and take a mouthful of food. "I can't believe I met Kat Saunders."

"She seems nice."

"Nice? Damn, Renny, she's amazing."

He laughs. "She's something all right."

"I totally fangirled."

Renny laughs harder. "Yeah, you did." I put my fork down. "Don't worry about it. I have a feeling we'll be seeing more of Kat."

Relieved, I pick my fork up again. "I hope so.

How's the food?"

"Thanks for giving me extra egg rolls."

"Destiny is right... you used to love them."

"I think I still do."

Smiling, I go back to my meal. The sun has about disappeared. Renny stands and turns on a light.

"Do you like being in Tourmaline?"

Renny shrugs. "It seems okay. It's nice to have Destiny close. The work at the garage keeps me busy, and Rush seems to think he can get me a nice settlement for my time in prison."

"Rush?"

"He's a lawyer, and Destiny works for him. Between them, they got me out."

Guilt once again rushes over me. The food in my mouth feels like sawdust, and swallowing it is easier with a large gulp of wine.

"I didn't tell you that to make you feel bad, Thea. I told you I forgave you. My life here is simple. I go to work, I go home, and I'm thankful for every breath of fresh air I take, but I'll be honest..." he puts down his bowl and stares me in the eyes, "... until I've paid Jackson, Steve, Hunter, Samuel, and Derrick a visit, I'm only existing. I *will* have my revenge, and they *will* pay."

His eyes appear darker. It might be the fading light, but a shiver runs up my spine.

Rubbing my arms, I stand and move away from him. "What do you need to know?"

"Steve is the only one I can't find."

My hands rest on the railing, and I stare down at them. "I have Hunter's number. I could call him and set up a meet?"

His chair moves back, and I feel him standing behind me. "No. I don't want you hurt."

Releasing a breath, I turn around. "How else are you going to find him?"

"A friend is looking into it."

He's far too close to me, so I skitter sideways to put some distance between us.

Renny frowns and takes a step toward me. "I'm not a danger to you, Thea. Zachary changes everything. You're his mother, and he needs you. I could never hurt the mother of my son."

My stomach sinks, and I wrap my arms around myself. That's all I am to Renny now, his son's mother. With a self-deprecating laugh, I turn back around. "Of course, for Zachary... your wrath is aimed at our old friends." Moving even farther away, I shuffle around the table, putting it between us. "I should get back."

"Thea—"

"I don't want to wear out my welcome with Destiny."

Renny moves around the table, closing the distance between us. "Well, that's something I wanted to talk to you about."

"You want us to leave?"

"No," he blurts.

"You want *me* to leave?"

"What? No. Thea, please sit." He pulls my chair out and gestures for me to sit. "I know this isn't a big city, but Tourmaline is safe. The people from our past wouldn't dare set foot in this town because of the Savage Angels, and I work for them."

"At the garage?"

"Yeah."

I take a seat and move my food around the bowl with the fork. "You want us to stay?"

"Yes," Renny replies. "And I can tell I'm fucking this up." He reaches over and touches my hand. "I want to get to know *you* again. There's nothing I want more than to build a relationship with *you* and our *son*. I've made a lot of mistakes, Thea. I don't want to make anymore. This here, now... it's all I care about."

Pulling my hand away, I stare into his eyes. "Except you want your pound of flesh. You want revenge, and Zachary and I can't be a part of that. I've kept him safe, and if it means I need to keep him safe from you, *I will.*"

Renny sits back. He nods. His lips are pressed together, and his eyes bore into mine. "They owe me, Thea, but if you stay here, none of it will blow back on you. Tourmaline is a nice town filled with good people. You could build a life here. We could all get a fresh start."

A new beginning.

Where once I dreamed about a life with Renny, then that dream turned into finding a safe place for Zachary, and now it feels like I've come full circle. A life with Renny and Zachary, but we can't be part of his world if he's chasing monsters.

"Only if you promise to let sleeping dogs lie." Reaching out, I grab his hand. "Please, Renny, can't you leave them alone?"

He leans forward, his lips inches from mine, and I think he's going to kiss me, but with a shake of his head, he says, "Not until they've paid for what they did."

My heart skips a beat, and I pull away from him. Renny hasn't learned a damn thing being in jail. He's the same old Renny, but this time, he's a twisted man who wants to hurt and punish.

"Take me home."

I stand and walk outside.

Once again, I'm wishing things were different, only this time, they can be.

Zachary and I don't need to stay around while Renny destroys everything around him.

CHAPTER 14

RENNY

Should I have lied to Thea? Probably. If I'm being honest with myself, I don't want to build a life with her and Zach built on deception. I want to share my plans with her so she isn't blindsided when I exact my revenge. Sitting so close to her, all I had to do was lean in and claim what I think is still mine, and maybe it'd be enough for her to forgive me when the time comes.

When I get outside, Thea is sitting in the car, staring straight ahead. I start the car and drive us to Destiny's.

Before I turn the car off, I say, "Wait there."

Getting out of the car, I jog around and open her door, then hold out my hand to Thea to help her slide out. She looks at my outstretched hand, then puts her hand in mine and glides out of the car.

Thea tugs on her hand, but I hold on to it and clutch it to my chest.

"Don't make any hasty decisions. Stay here, keep your job, and let's get to know each other again."

Thea opens her mouth and then closes it. She tries to speak again, but nothing comes out, and she pulls on her hand. Without thinking, keeping her hand on my chest, I pull her toward me with my other hand, cupped to the back of her head.

I brush my lips against Thea's, tentative and feather-soft, as I gently massage the back of her neck. She gasps, and an electric current sends a shiver down my spine. Ever so slightly, I deepen the kiss, pressing my lips more firmly against hers, and as though it were yesterday, we find our rhythm. Heads angled, noses brushing against each other, I sink into her.

Thea's hand reaches up and cradles the side of my face, her fingers grazing along my jawline. Slowly, our lips part, her breath warm and shallow against my mouth. Diving in again, the kiss intensifies, and our mouths press more urgently as we rekindle our passion for each other. With lips soft and warm, my arm wraps around her, and our bodies meld together. My tongue teases hers as they meet in a delicate dance of exploration. Sinking deeper into the kiss, I'm lost in her warmth and closeness and my growing fervor. My pulse races as Thea clutches me closer to her, and this feeling of rightness washes over me.

Thea breaks the kiss and turns her head to the side. "No," she whispers so softly, I almost don't hear it.

With my forehead pressed to her temple, I nod. This is all too fast, and we have a long way to go before I can claim her. Using all my willpower, I let her go and step back.

Thea's beautiful hazel eyes find mine. "I've missed you, Renny, but I'm not a kid anymore. I've got responsibilities. Zachary depends on me, and I can't let him down." Stumbling, she all but runs from me into the house, and I wish I could go after her to finish what we started. But she's right. There's more to our story than just us.

Zach.

He deserves better.

And for him, I *will* do better.

It's barely daylight when I start work at the garage. There was no sleep for me after kissing Thea. My hard-on barely subsided even when I relieved myself in the shower. It was her face I imagined, and her body I wish I were spilling my seed into.

No one else is here, so I get to work finishing up the two cars that are on lifts.

At nine, Zeke wanders in and sees me sitting on a bench covered in grease.

"Where are the two cars?" he asks as he sits next to me.

"Done. Came in early."

"You finished both?"

"Yeah, moved them outside. Didn't you see them?"

Zeke shrugs. "I'm half asleep, man. I need coffee. Can I buy you a cup?"

"At the café?"

"Sure." He glances around. "There's nothing left for us to do today. We could go for a ride?"

An idea occurs to me. "The Cherry?"

"You want to spend the day at a strip club?"

"Yeah. I want to talk to Tobias."

Zeke stands and chuckles. "Should have known. Was it all that time in prison? Did you swap sides?"

"Fuck you."

"Hey, I'm not judging. I like vaginas, but Tobias is pretty. Is it the long hair?"

"Don't be an ass." I know Zeke is kidding. Well, I hope he is. "He has information for me."

"Do you ride?"

"It's been a while, but it's like a bike, yeah? You never forget."

"We are talking motorbikes, not..." Zeke quirks

an eyebrow at me.

Ignoring him, I stand. "Is there a bike I can borrow?"

Zeke laughs. "Yeah, she ain't pretty, though."

"Don't need her to be."

"Go shower. Looking the way you do, Tobias won't let you sit in his office, let alone in the building."

"He is a pretty boy."

"Yep, I knew it. Batting for the other team."

With a shake of my head, I walk into the locker room and head for the showers.

The Cherry is nothing like I imagined. It's a long, narrow building with no windows and a single solid wood door at the front. Zeke parks on the street, and I park the bike I've borrowed next to his. It's an ugly bike with mismatched parts and a worn and ripped seat that has seen better days.

Zeke climbs off his bike and jumps up and down a few times. "How'd she run?"

"She might be ugly, but she runs smooth."

"It's a Frankenstein. We make them out of old bikes, do them up, make them pretty, and sell them.

You'd be surprised how much they sell for when they're pretty."

No, I wouldn't. I'm sure there's a huge market for motorcycles made by the Savage Angels MC. There are a lot of wannabes who pay a pretty penny to say they've got a genuine Savage Angels' bike.

Zeke pounds on the door to The Cherry and waits, his hands on his hips, staring intently at the closed door. Eventually, he turns around and looks up at a camera, waving his arms in the air. "Come on, Tobias. Let us in."

As if on cue, the door opens, and Rebel steps out. "Why are you here?"

"My new friend here..." he points at me, "... wants to see Tobias. Is he here?"

"Is he ever *not* here?" Rebel replies sarcastically.

Zeke doesn't answer, walks inside, and I follow him.

"Hey, Rebel."

"Hey, Renny. What did you want with Tobias?"

Not wanting to share with him, I say, "Just wanted to see where my sister once worked."

"Damn, Destiny was the best."

I stop walking and turn to face him. Realization goes over his face as he thinks about what he said about my sister.

"Aww, shit. I'm sorry, man. I didn't mean anything by it. Destiny was the top strip... I mean, performer here when she... ah... performed."

Taking a deep breath, I look him in the eyes, shake my head, and double-time it to catch up with Zeke.

"What did Rebel want?"

"To take his foot out of his damn mouth."

Zeke frowns but keeps walking. "Sounds like Rebel."

Zeke takes me into the depths of The Cherry. Tucked away in a corner is a black door with a single word in faded letters etched across its weathered surface—*Staff*. Zeke glances over his shoulder, then turns the knob. The heavy door creaks open to reveal a dimly lit hallway that seems to stretch endlessly. Our footsteps echo down the long corridor as we walk past a succession of identical doors, their dark wood scuffed and scratched with use. Each one is closed tightly, keeping hidden secrets beyond our reach. At the end of the passage, I make out the ghostly red glow of an exit sign.

As we pass by the row of identical doors, I note one that stands out from the rest with a tarnished brass plaque in engraved letters that reads—*Manager*. Zeke's pace slows as we approach it. His knuckles rap against the wooden door once, the sound echoing sharply in the deserted hallway.

We linger there for a heartbeat, Zeke's eyes meeting mine briefly before his hand turns the knob. The door swings inward with a faint creak, revealing a dim office. At the far end sits a heavy oak desk, and behind it is a silhouette I recognize instantly as Tobias. His hands are steepled neatly in front of him, an imitation of deep thought. But his eyes are keen and alert, watching us closely. He shows no surprise as if he had been expecting our arrival.

Along the wall behind him, six television monitors glow. Their flickering screens display crisp black-and-white security footage of the club. The televisions' pale lights cast Tobias' angular features in an eerie high-contrast glow. He surveys us without a word, leaning back leisurely in his leather chair. His confidence unnerves me, and I am hyperaware of each shadowed corner and camera lens following our every move.

Zeke steps forward. "How the fuck are you, Tobias? Is business good?"

Tobias stands, his face breaking into a smile as he extends a hand to Zeke. "I'm good, brother. And business is always excellent. It's what you pay me to do."

"Not me, man,... that'd be Dane."

"Renny, how are you?"

"Good. Nice place you have here."

"It's not mine. I take care of it for the Savage Angels."

"Yeah, but he runs it like it's his," Zeke says.

"I try. What can I do you for?"

I glance at Zeke, unsure if I can talk in front of him. “Ahh… you were going to track down a name for me?”

Zeke doesn’t speak, but his eyes narrow, and he folds his arms across his chest.

Tobias notices his stance and cocks his head to the side. “Zeke, would you mind giving us a minute?”

Zeke purses his lips and glances from Tobias to me. “I’ll be out front with Rebel.” He saunters out of the office, shutting the door firmly behind him.

“You’d do worse than to trust Zeke. He’s a good man with a good heart.”

“I know, but why get him involved when I don’t have to?”

Tobias nods, opens a drawer, and holds out a piece of paper. “He’ll be at this address tomorrow night at eleven. It’s a club, and it doesn’t open until nine. He has people everywhere, and they all probably know what you look like. Good luck getting the jump on him.”

“You misunderstand me, Tobias. I’m not going to kill him. All I want is a conversation.”

His eyebrows go up in surprise. “Still, he isn’t going to sit down with you quietly.”

“He will. Steve is going to be curious about what I want.”

“No, Steve will want the money. Do you still have it?”

Surprised he even knows about it, I say, "Yeah. But it's complicated."

"Matters of revenge always are."

Holding the piece of paper in the air, I smile, "Thank you for this."

Turning, I open the door to his office, shut it, and retrace my steps. Zeke is sitting at a table with Rebel, and they both turn and watch me approach.

"Did you get what you wanted?" Zeke asks.

"Yeah."

Zeke slaps Rebel on the shoulder. "See ya, man. Good luck getting Ruby to forgive you."

Rebel's face clouds over, and he nods. "Yeah, I'm in the shit."

Laughing, Zeke says, "That's 'cause you *are* shit." He laughs at his own joke. "See ya, wouldn't want to be ya."

Rebel looks miserable as he gives Zeke the bird. Zeke blows him a kiss, and we head for the front of The Cherry.

"Make sure you shut the door on your way out," Rebel yells.

"Will do." Zeke opens the door, gestures for me to walk out, then slams it behind us. "He's in deep with his old lady. If you want some more ink, she's a hell of a tattooist." He pulls up the sleeve of his T-shirt, exposing more of his arm. "She did this whole sleeve."

It's impressive work. Maybe not as good as mine, but there's no doubt the woman has skills.

"He seems a little..."

"Weird?"

"Yeah."

"Rebel will never be anything but a soldier in the MC. He's loyal, the guy you want to have next to you in a fight, but he's odd. His woman, Ruby, is super sweet. The MC helped set her up in Tourmaline, and she has a tattoo shop in town. The tourists book her a year in advance." Zeke rubs his face. "To be honest, I've been waiting for her to kick his ass to the curb, but she seems to love the jerk."

"You like her?"

"No. I've got a woman, Cassia. I guess I think Ruby could do better."

I put a leg over the bike and nod. It's how I think about Thea and me. Even when we were younger, I always thought she could have done better. Thea had dreams and goals, and I ruined all of them. I might have been in a cage, but she was in one too. I understand those feelings. Relationships are complex, and maybe Ruby and Thea see things Rebel, Zeke, and I don't. Perhaps Thea stayed because she cared about me despite the challenges. The past can't be changed, but I now have an opportunity to rebuild our relationship into something stronger.

Zeke starts his bike, as do I.

Taking a deep breath, I pull away from The Cherry.

It's a beautiful day, and soon, the things in my nightmares will be dead and buried.

CHAPTER 15

RENNY

The throbbing bass pulses through the darkened club as bodies gyrate on the crowded dance floor. Strobe lights flash erratically, revealing glimpses of the revelers—some dressed in barely-there outfits, others wearing baggy jeans low on their hips. The air is thick with the scent of sweat, alcohol, and smoke swirling from the fog machines. In the shadows, groups lean against the bar, knocking back shots and yelling to be heard over the deafening electronic dance music.

The bartenders pour drinks as fast as they can, not checking IDs too closely. Underneath the bar, deals are made, and baggies are exchanged discreetly. On the fringes, loners scope out potential partners for the night, men with hungry eyes and women in tight dresses sizing each other up. In the dark corners, couples grind against each other or make out, hands roaming. Furtive glances dart around, ever watchful for those who might object.

More than one server has tried to strike up a conversation but moved on when I made it clear I wasn't interested. It's nearly midnight when Steve walks into the club. He has a woman on each arm, the types who wear too much makeup and have a permanently bored expression on their faces. He appears older but, judging by the women, not wiser. He makes a show of saying hello to people as he passes, proving he's the *big man*. All the while, he's getting closer and closer to me. When he's about six feet away, he kisses both women and sends them on their way, then tilts his head side to side, and if we weren't in a club with music pumping, I'd be able to hear the bones cracking. It's an old habit he used to do as a kid. Steve rolls his shoulders back and looks directly at me, his mouth curling into a sly half-smile. He knew I was here the whole time.

"Renny!" He holds his arms out wide. "It's been a long time. What, five?" He takes a step toward me. "Six?" And another. "No, seven?"

I put down my beer and smile. "Eight, going on nine."

He grins and paces in front of me. "That's right. Yeah, you went to prison for murder."

A woman standing near me glances my way and then shifts.

"I did. But we both know I didn't do it."

"Do we? Do we, really?" Steve laughs. It's a hollow, fake sound and completely theatrical.

"How about we go outside and talk about this?"

Steve shakes his whole body. "Go outside with you? A convicted murderer? I don't think so." His face morphs into a mask of fear, but it's all for show.

"Cut the crap, Steve. If I were going to kill you, I would've waited outside, in the shadows, and you would never have seen me coming."

He stands next to me, elbows resting on the bar. "Fine. What do you want, Renny?"

"I want to know why. You were like family, and together, I thought we were building toward a common goal."

Steve barks out a laugh. "Is that what you think? Jesus, Renny, it was your way or the damn highway. I never wanted to work nine to five. Never wanted to be a sap working for minimum wage, but you wouldn't listen. We tried to tell you."

"Like fuck you did."

Steve twists to stare me in the eyes. "We did. The night we boosted the money. The rest of us wanted to split and go our separate ways, but you wouldn't hear of it. Said we needed to sit on it so the powers that be wouldn't get suspicious."

"We boosted money off a drug cartel. Did it occur

to you they might come looking for us?"

"How? No one saw us. Hell, no one saw anything." He smiles. "You still have the money, don't you?"

I don't answer his question, but instead, I say, "So you let Samuel butcher innocents and frame me for it?"

He claps his hands together. "Yep, and if you'd only brought the money with you like you were supposed to do, I'd be living in Mexico and having a hell of a life."

"Wow! You were always a dreamer, but I didn't realize you were delusional."

"And that's why we won. That's why you went to jail. And why we didn't."

"You think *you won*?"

Steve's eyebrows draw together, and he shrugs. "Well, none of us spent time in the pen. I'd call it a win." He stares past me and lifts his chin in a greeting. Following his gaze, I see my four old friends.

"It's a party now." Steve smirks.

Copying him, I look out into the throng of people on the dance floor and nod at Judge. Six other members of the Savage Angels melt out of the crowd, moving toward us—seven men, all with an air of danger.

Steve tracks their movements, and I say, "It sure is. Wanna dance?"

"You really want to start something? There's a room *full* of eyewitnesses, and with your record, who do you think the police will believe?"

Moving closer to him, so close I can smell the sweat and fear, I whisper, "I. Was. Innocent."

"No one is ever *truly* innocent."

Turning to stare back where the others were standing, they're no longer there. "Seems your friends have abandoned you."

"They were your family once too."

"Yeah, and look where they got me."

"Tell me, Renny, how is Thea? And your son? You know we wouldn't have been able to pin it on you if it wasn't for her. She held up her end of the deal."

My hand contracts into a fist. I pull it back and hit him in the jaw. It makes a thumping sound, and the expression on Steve's face is priceless. He staggers backward, wiping the blood off his mouth, then yells as he charges toward me.

His arms wrap around my waist, and he throws me to the floor. Lips peeled back, Steve lifts his foot to stamp on my face, but I roll away. Bouncers emerge from the crowd, but the Savage Angels hold them back.

Rising quickly to my feet, Steve and I circle each other. He spits blood onto the floor and wipes his face with the back of his hand.

"I can't believe you still have a hard-on for that bitch."

"Don't fucking talk about her," I snarl.

"You know... we told her we were going to split the money with her. It's the only reason she helped us."

"So holding a knife to her belly and threatening *our* child, *my* child, was all for show?"

Steve laughs loudly. "Can't blame a guy for trying? But we were going to split it with her. Well, we told ourselves we were." He lunges at me, throwing a fist up high, which I duck, but his other hand hits me in the kidneys. With a groan, I move back a step, then hit him twice in the face and once in the jaw in quick succession.

Steve goes down.

Out cold.

Judge places a hand on my shoulder, and I twirl out of his grasp, fists raised, ready to defend myself.

"Easy, Renny, it's me." Judge's hands are raised, palms out. "We've gotta move. One of the bouncers called the cops."

Fury courses through my veins as I storm toward the club's exit, Judge and Zeke close on my heels. The heavy beat of the music thumps in time with the adrenaline pounding in my ears. We shove through the writhing crowd, their laughing faces blurring together in my rage.

A bouncer at the door jumps back at the fire in my eyes, and in seconds, we burst out into the cold night air. I can still feel the imprint of Steve's fist colliding with my side. The outrage begs me to turn back, to make him pay. But the club or the streets are no place for retribution.

Not yet.

For now, we regroup.

Judge claps a hand on my shoulder, solidarity in his steely gaze.

Zeke cracks his knuckles menacingly.

Tonight was only a warning, but I don't back down easy.

My old crew started this fire, but I'll be the one to finish it.

CHAPTER 16

THEA

Staring at the empty coffee pot, I mechanically refill it and look around the café. It's two in the afternoon, and it feels like this day will never end. I can't concentrate. My mind keeps going back to the kiss Renny and I shared a week ago. Sighing, I lean against the counter, remembering the feel of his hand gently cupping my head, his fingertips massaging my neck, sending tingles down my spine, and how my heart pounded when his lips first met mine in a soft, perfect kiss. I can't stop smiling as I relive every detail—the scratch of his stubble lightly grazing my chin, the sweet taste of his lips, and that lingering moment when we both didn't want the kiss to end.

Glancing at the clock, I still have an hour before my shift ends and, hopefully, seeing Renny again.

He's avoided me, waiting until after I've gone to work to see Zachary and leaving before I get home, but today, Howie said I could finish up early. It's been hard to focus on work all week as I replay the kiss in my mind.

"Earth to Thea. Are you in there?" asks Howie.

"Geez, sorry, boss. Did you need something?"

Howie shakes his head. "I said you can clock out early if you want."

Not needing to hear him ask me twice, I reach under the counter, grab my purse, and head for the door. It's Wednesday, and I don't have to be back at work until Friday.

"Have a good day tomorrow," I call over my shoulder.

It's a short walk home to Destiny and Kade's. There are no cars parked in the driveway as I walk the path to the front door.

Opening it wide, I yell, "I'm home."

Silence greets me.

"Is anyone here?" Standing in the foyer, I listen for sounds of life, but it's clear no one is here.

With a sigh, I trudge up the stairs to the room I share with Zachary.

Destiny has left a pile of clothes neatly folded on our bed. I put them away, keeping sweatpants and a T-shirt out, and head for the bathroom.

After three hours, the house is still empty.

On the stove, I've got a Bolognese sauce simmering, and garlic bread sits ready for the oven. I spent time curling my hair into soft waves and putting on mascara and lip gloss. It's been a while since I tried to look this nice.

I'm listening to Luke Combs sing "Fast Car" on my cell phone, although I prefer Tracy Chapman's version. I'm singing to myself, stirring the sauce, and wondering where everyone is at this hour.

"Mom, you sound like a wounded cat."

Turning around, Zachary and Renny are there grinning at me.

"How long have you two been standing there?"

"Not long." Renny moves to stand next to me and sticks his finger in my sauce.

"Renny! It's hot."

He winks and puts his finger in his mouth. "Tastes good."

"Where have you been?"

Renny leans against the counter and points at Zachary. "We went for a drive to Pearl County. I wanted to show Zach the school over there."

Frowning, I ask, "Aren't there any schools in Tourmaline?"

Zach sits on a stool at the kitchen island. "Of course, they have schools here, Mom. But Dad thought I might want to go to a bigger school. He said we could live in Pearl if we wanted."

"Your dad and I haven't had a conversation about schools or even if we'll move here." I quickly look at Renny.

"I was only giving him options. The decision will be up to you. *If* you decide to stay, it wouldn't bother me if you lived here in town or in Pearl. It's not like it's a huge drive."

"Do you want us to stay?" asks Zachary.

"Yes." Renny doesn't hesitate while staring straight at me. "I want you near me." Then he looks at Zachary. "But if you go back to your old place, I'll come visit every chance I get."

Zachary smiles and says, "I like it here."

"I do too."

"Can we stay?" Zachary shouts.

Glancing at Renny, I say, "Mia called today… our old landlord wants his rent for this month. He told Mia if I'm not coming back, he has someone ready to move into our old apartment."

"Who's Mia?"

"She was our neighbor. Mia watched me when Mom worked nights," explains Zachary.

"She's a good friend and convinced our landlord

to give me 'til the end of next week to pay him."

Renny nods and points at Zachary. "Hey, bud, why don't you go get cleaned up for dinner?"

Zachary smiles and climbs off the stool. "Mom makes the best Bolognese."

Renny's eyes go to the ceiling, and he listens for Zachary's footsteps up the stairs before he speaks, "Do you have enough for the rent?" He pulls a pan off a shelf and fills it with hot water for the pasta. "And would you like to stay here in Tourmaline?"

"No, on the rent, but I'll figure something out. And yes, it'd be good for Zachary to be near you."

"What about you? Do you want to be near me again, Thea?"

My breath catches in my throat.

Renny has his eyes on the pan of water that he's put on the stove.

"Y-yes," I stammer.

A smile spreads across his face, and Renny moves quickly to engulf me in a hug. "I'm so glad."

"What smells so good?" asks Destiny as she walks into the kitchen.

Renny releases me and smiles at his sister. "Thea made dinner."

Destiny slides her briefcase on a stool, puts her face over the sauce, and inhales. "Damn, it smells good. Kade won't be home until late, and I'm starving. Let's eat."

"Renny, would you find me some bowls?"

He winks at me and opens a cupboard.

Destiny opens the refrigerator and pulls out a bottle of wine. "Renny, can you find us some wine glasses?" Destiny asks as she opens the bottle.

For the next few minutes, we are all busy in the kitchen. Renny sets the table, and Destiny pours us both a glass of wine while I put the garlic bread in the oven and cook the pasta.

"How was your day at work?" asks Destiny.

"Good. Howie is a great boss. He lets me keep my tips, doesn't try to touch my ass, and he's funny."

"Doesn't try to touch your ass?" Renny frowns. "Does that happen often?"

"Yep. For some reason, coworkers and customers seem to think my ass is public property. But don't worry, they only do it once."

Destiny giggles. "Girrrlll, I hear you."

We share a knowing look, and Renny scratches the side of his head in confusion. Zachary walks back into the kitchen and sits at the dining table next to Destiny.

I hand the garlic bread to Renny, who puts it in the center of the table while I walk over with two bowls of spaghetti Bolognese, which I put down in front of Zachary and Destiny. When I turn around, Renny has a bowl in each hand and brings them to the table.

"Thank you."

He winks at me, and my stomach flutters. "Thank

you for cooking."

We sit opposite Zachary and Destiny, our legs brushing against each other.

This feels good.

It feels like a home.

I have a fork full of pasta and sauce when I hear the front door open.

"Yo! Destiny, you home?"

"In here," Destiny yells back but doesn't get up.

A man walks in, wearing a Savage Angels MC cut with tattoos down both arms. "Is there enough for me?" he asks, walking to the stove.

Destiny stands and walks over to him. "Go sit. I'll fix you a plate."

He smiles and sits at the head of the table, extending his hand to me. "I'm Zeke, and you must be Thea and Zach."

I shake his hand and nod. "Yes, I am."

He holds out his hand to Zachary, who puts down his fork, shakes his hand, and says, "Nice to meet you."

Destiny puts a bowl in front of him. He immediately reaches out, grabs two slices of garlic bread, and dips it into the sauce.

"Cassia can't cook to save her soul. I miss home cooking. At least when I lived with Dirt, he'd cook, but Cass, nope."

Destiny laughs. "*You* could cook."

Zeke stuffs a slice of bread into his mouth and

makes a humming noise. “Oh, man. This is good.”

“Thank you.”

Zeke looks at me. “You made this?” His eyes flick to Renny. “She’s a keeper.”

Renny puts an arm across the back of my chair. “She sure is.”

My insides now have more than flutters, and my face heats, which means I’m probably beetroot red.

Zeke stands, gets a wine glass, and pours some wine. “Where’s Kade?”

“The Cherry.” Destiny grabs a piece of garlic bread. “He’s working the late shift, making sure everyone gets out okay.”

“Problems?”

Destiny shakes her head. “I don’t think so. You know how Tobias can be.”

Their conversation continues, but I pay little attention to it. My entire focus is on Renny and his body touching mine.

Zeke slaps the table as he takes a huge mouthful of pasta and sauce and makes a face, which I’m sure is supposed to resemble bliss, but he ends up looking ridiculous.

“You can cook for me anytime.”

Renny shakes his head. “Get your woman to cook for you. This one’s taken.”

Not sure where to look or what to say, I take a mouthful of pasta and keep my eyes averted to the wooden dining table.

"Mom cooks like this all the time. She says it's cheaper than takeout. And she always cooks too much so we can have leftovers the next day."

"Your mom is smart." Zeke nods.

"Yeah, she is, but sometimes it's nice to have takeout."

"We have takeout."

Zachary rolls his eyes. "The first Friday of every month, I'm allowed to pick what we have. Last month, I picked pizza."

"Once a month you get takeout?" asks Destiny, staring at me.

"It's a treat for Zachary. I'd eat the same thing every day, but he likes variety."

Destiny glances at Renny, and they exchange some unspoken words. I'm a little confused, but she quickly smiles at me.

"You have to tell me how you made this."

"The trick is to let it simmer for a couple of hours. All day is better. And if you have someone who doesn't like vegetables, grate them up and mix them in." I point my fork at Zachary. "They'll never know, and it bulks out the sauce."

Zachary uses his fork to inspect his meal, then shrugs and keeps eating. "Tastes good."

"Because *vegetables* are good for you," I chide.

Zachary rolls his eyes again but doesn't backchat me.

"So, are you two going to stay in Tourmaline?"

Zachary stops chewing, fixing an expectant gaze on me.

I place my fork down and turn my attention to Zeke. "Yeah, I think we are."

"Yes!" Zachary stands, runs around the table, and hugs me. "You are the best, Mom."

Laughing, I put my arms around him. "You say that now."

"Can we live here with Aunty Destiny and Uncle Kade?"

Glancing at Destiny, I say, "For a little while, but we'll need a place of our own." Zachary walks back to his seat. "Is it easy to find a rental in Tourmaline?"

"I'll ask around. But you two are welcome to stay here as long as you need." Destiny reaches out and picks up a slice of garlic bread.

"What about your old apartment?" asks Zeke. "You must have belongings and shit you want to bring here?"

"Zeke, language!" admonishes Destiny.

"Sorry. I meant to say *stuff*."

Zachary giggles. "We don't have a lot of stuff."

He's right, we don't, mainly because we've moved so many times. Everything important to me, like Zachary's baby photographs, is packed in the suitcase upstairs. I learned long ago not to get attached to things.

Zeke is watching me, and I say, "We have a few

things. But Zachary is right. We could move everything we own in the trunk of someone's car."

"*Damn*, woman. You are just about perfect. You can cook and don't waste money on material things. If you ever get sick of Mr. Broody over there, let me know."

Renny leans forward. "I'm telling Cassia you said that."

Zeke feigns a pained expression. "Low blow, brother."

"Yeah, well, stop trying to steal Thea."

"I'm only saying I know more than one man who would kill to have a woman like Thea. I didn't necessarily mean myself."

"Nice try, Zeke." Destiny laughs.

Zeke screws up his face, and Destiny laughs harder. I'm laughing when Renny's hand lands on my leg under the table, and I nearly jump out of my chair.

"What?" asks Zeke, scanning the room for threats.

Embarrassed, I say, "Nothing. Just got a chill."

"It's warm," Zeke states.

"You know that feeling when someone walks over your grave?"

"Yeah?"

"Well, that." I pick up my fork and continue to eat.

Renny laughs, and I sneak a glance at him. It's

like old times. When we were younger, Renny could quicken my pulse faster than any workout or fright. His eyes have turned the warm hue of whiskey, and this perfect moment feels too good to be real.

This house has turned into our home and this town into our sanctuary.

CHAPTER 17

RENNY

My plans for my former crew are in motion.

In prison, I became friends with the ruthless Juarez Cartel we had stolen money from. At one point, their notorious leader, Sergio Alvarez, did time in Glenford. I saved his life during a bloody war between rival prison factions. He owes me but doesn't know my face was behind the three-million-dollar heist. For a while, we shared a cramped cell. The guards expected us to kill each other, but I had bigger aspirations. It was difficult to prove my trustworthiness to the skeptical kingpin. But after I saved his life in the exercise yard, fending off a shiv attack with my bare hands, Sergio began to confide in me.

He told me about the missing money and the many informants he had tortured and killed trying to find it. He was obsessed with getting revenge against the mysterious thief.

After my tense run-in with Steve, I contacted Sergio from a burner phone. I claimed I'd heard a rumor on the prison grapevine about a guy bragging in a bar about how he and his crew cleverly stole millions from the cartel. It was simple—Tobias tracked down Steve's address, and one night, when he was out, I broke in and stashed the original grimy money bags in an air conditioning vent.

All I need to do now is wait.

The cartel and Sergio will do my dirty work for me.

They will wipe out those five names on my list without me having to lift a finger. Sergio even offered me a finder's fee, which I turned down.

Their lives for eight years in jail is payment enough.

Thea and I have been seeing each other for a week. It's been lots of kissing and touching, but I don't want to push her too hard, too fast.

Today, we are driving back to her old apartment to collect her things. She's also paying her landlord the rent she owes plus two weeks and giving him notice to vacate. Destiny once again lent us her truck and is looking after Zach.

Thea is sitting up against me, her hand on my thigh, telling me about her neighbors at her old place. They sound like good people.

"We could stay overnight?"

"Really?" she asks.

"Yeah. Destiny has Zach—"

"And is spoiling him rotten."

I grin. "Yep. She says she's got lots of catching up to do. This way, you can spend some time with Mia, and she can meet me."

From the little I know of Mia, she has been a good friend to Thea and finds it strange that Zachary's father is back in the picture, having been absent for so long.

"I haven't told her much about you."

"I figured." I thread my fingers with Thea's. "Besides, this way, we get to spend some time together alone." I raise her hand to my lips and kiss it.

Thea gasps, and her face is becoming a pretty shade of pink.

"I didn't think of that."

"So, you don't want to spend time alone with me?" I tease.

She wiggles closer and shakes her head. "It's not that." Thea rests her head on my shoulder. "But I'm not fourteen anymore."

Laughing, I say, "Well, that's good 'cause if you were, I could get arrested."

Thea rubs her thumb over my knuckles. "I guess what I'm trying to say is my body has changed. I had a baby, I'm older... what if you..."

Again, I kiss the back of her hand. "We've both changed. You are prettier now than you were then and far sexier. Woman, I've had a boner since you got in the truck and sat next to me. In fact, this whole week has been torture."

"Really?" Thea whispers, her eyes wide.

Grabbing her hand, I put it on my cock and groan. "Really."

Thea moves and kisses my neck. "We could pull over?"

Laughing, I say, "No. I want to do this right. In a bed, somewhere private. You're right, we're not teenagers anymore, and I want to take my time."

She sits back next to me and smiles. "You *like* me."

"I do."

Like isn't a strong enough word, but it's far too early in our relationship for words of love. We are still getting to know each other, and I don't want to frighten her off.

"I like you too."

"I know."

"How?"

"The noises you make when I kiss you, how you smile at me when no one is looking, and, most of all, how you treat me in front of our son."

Glancing down at Thea, she practically melts. Her face goes soft, and she smiles, snuggling even closer to me.

"He's really come out of his shell around you. I noticed he showed you his artwork." I nod. "He never shares that with anyone. Not even his friends from school."

"Why?"

Thea lifts a shoulder, shrugging. "I think it's because he went to a museum with his class, saw some paintings, and felt his didn't measure up."

"But he's good."

"I know. But he has no self-confidence where his art is concerned."

It surprises me he doesn't think he's good enough. For a kid, he shows talent. With practice and instruction, he could turn it into a profession.

"I guess, together, we'll have to work on that."

Thea sits up and kisses my cheek.

"What was that for?"

"For being you. For understanding our son and taking us in when you didn't have to. I wouldn't have blamed you, Renny, if you never wanted to speak to me again."

Not wanting to destroy our feeling of closeness in the truck but needing her to understand, I say, "I was mad at you for a long time. Your face and the others, well, I'd picture what I was going to say and do to you all, over and over again. The day I spoke to you outside your building?"

"Yes?"

"It wasn't the first time I'd seen you and Zach. The moment I laid eyes on him, I knew he was mine, and maybe subconsciously, I understood why you did what you did. I wish I'd known sooner."

Thea makes a noise, and I squeeze her hand tighter.

"Don't feel bad. What happened with the guys and you… that's *all* on me. I put you in that position. I was young and reckless with the most precious thing in the world… *you*."

"Renny," Thea's voice is all breathy. "I think we're both to blame."

"Maybe we need to start all over with forgiveness." I glance down at her. "And no secrets."

Thea raises my hand to her soft lips. "No secrets," she utters the words against my skin like a prayer.

CHAPTER 18

THEA

Mia is waiting for me on the sidewalk when we pull up. The truck has barely stopped before I'm out and hugging her.

"Girl, I've missed you!" Mia holds on to me just as tightly. She leans back and holds me at arm's length. "Are you okay?"

"I'm better than okay." I grab her hand and drag her around the truck. "Mia, this is Renny, Zachary's father."

She does a double-take and extends her hand to him. "Nice to meet you."

Renny dips his chin and uses both hands to shake hers. "I've heard so many nice things about you."

Mia glances at me. "I wish I could say the same."

Renny releases her and pulls me into his side,

pressing his lips to my temple. "Why don't you two catch up, and I'll get the bags?"

"Okay. We're on the third floor, apartment 318."

Mia links her arm with mine, and we walk together through the entry and up the stairs. By the time we get to our floor, I'm breathing hard, but Mia looks like she took a leisurely stroll.

"You're leaving, aren't you?"

"Yes."

"To be with him?"

"Yes, and no. He lives in a small town called Tourmaline."

"I've heard of it. It's one of those places where the population swells in winter for skiing."

"Yep. I've got a job, and we're searching for a place to rent. The schools seem good, and Zachary has a man in his life. I think it's important for him to have that... he's missed out on so much."

"Girl, that's bullshit. That boy hasn't missed out on a damn thing. *You* made sure of that."

As I unlock and open the front door to my apartment, a scene of destruction awaits inside. Stepping into the living room, my eyes widen at the chaotic mess—the once pristine blue fabric of my couch is slashed open in multiple places, with chunks of foam sticking out of the gashes like bloated innards. Tufts of white feathers from the shredded throw pillows are scattered across the hardwood floor like fresh snow, covering any traces of the perpetrator. Turning slowly, I take in the rest of the upended room—books pulled from shelves, picture frames knocked over, and various belongings ransacked. A cold chill runs through me as I realize someone has broken in and ravaged my home while I was away. My heart pounds as I continue surveying the damage, dreading what else I might find disturbed or destroyed within the other rooms. The sense of violation at seeing my personal space so crudely invaded leaves me shaken and unsettled.

Renny comes through the door with a bag in each hand, then freezes as he takes in the chaotic scene.

Mia puts an arm around me. "Jesus, who would have done this? It doesn't even look like anything is missing."

"You were never a great housekeeper, but this seems extreme." He drops the bags and smiles. "We'll clean it up."

Mia puts her hands on her hips. "This isn't funny."

"No, it's not. But if you don't laugh, you'll cry," Renny speaks directly to me.

"We should call the police." Mia pulls her cell phone out of her pocket.

Renny shakes his head. "No point. You said yourself, nothing's been taken. This was a warning."

"They've trashed her home. Whoever *they are,* they should be punished."

Putting a hand over Mia's, I say, "Renny is right. Everything important to me was with me." Looking around, I shake my head. "This is all just... *stuff.*"

"Girl, are you serious?" She turns to face Renny. "And how do you know nothing has been taken?"

"Has anything been taken?" he asks me.

"I don't think so, but I haven't checked the rest of my apartment."

Renny moves past us checks Zachary's room, then mine, and smiles. "Seems like they only did this out here. The bedrooms look untouched."

Following him, I'm glad to see our mattresses are not torn up or the rooms ransacked. "Why would they only do this out here?"

"Maybe they were disturbed?" Renny stares at Mia. "Have you heard anything strange?"

"Strange?"

"Loud noises or people coming and going?"

"No, but let me go ask Tyrone." Mia steps back out into the hallway.

Renny pulls me in for a hug. "Are you okay?"

"You seem like you were expecting this."

He leans back. "Kind of. Seems like something they would do."

Pushing him back, I say, "You could have warned me."

"And I could have been wrong. Worrying you

over something that might not have happened didn't seem right." His hands splay out at his sides. "The main thing is, you weren't here when they were looking for you. This is nothing more than a temper tantrum, probably executed by Samuel."

"You're sure?"

Renny puts his hands on my shoulders. "Who else would do this? It has to be the old crew."

He is right. It has to be the old crew. But as I survey the wreckage in my apartment, a swell of anger rises within me. My heart aches at seeing the destruction. The thrift store couch Mia and I meticulously scrubbed, repaired, and reupholstered together is now ruined. The hours of elbow grease we put into restoring it is gone in an instant. I realize now that even these secondhand items, these bits and pieces I collected paycheck by paycheck, mean more than I thought. They represent my hard work, my style, and my memories, and someone has violated it all. The anger smolders, tinged with sadness. This was my haven, my space—imperfect—but mine. Seeing it ransacked stings deep in ways I never imagined.

Nodding, I move out of his embrace, open a closet, and pull out a broom and vacuum. Renny takes the broom and starts sweeping the feathers into a corner. Bending, I pick up the few books I had on a shelf and put them back, then turn our small coffee table over. One leg has been damaged, and it wobbles, then falls as it gives way.

Mia and Tyrone appear before me.

His eyes widen at the mess. “Damn. I’m so sorry, Thea.”

“It’s okay. It won’t take long to c-clean up.” My voice cracks, and I dip my chin to my chest to stop the tears.

Tyrone bends and picks up a piece of broken glass. “I noticed one of your plants was smashed in the alley, maybe three nights ago? I knew it was yours, as you keep them in the same blue and white pots. Anyway, I knocked on your door. There was no answer. Maybe I scared him?”

“Maybe.”

Renny moves closer to me and extends a hand to Tyrone. “I’m Renny Bennett.”

“I know you. You just got out of prison. They say you’re innocent.”

Mia frowns and points a finger at me. “Is that why you never said who Zachary’s father was? Because he was in prison?”

“He didn’t do it, Mia.”

“Is all this mess because of him?” I glance at Renny. “Well, that look tells me all I need to know. Girl, what are you doing?”

Renny holds up a hand to Mia. “The people who put me in jail did this. Mia, I promise you, Thea and Zach are safe. I won’t let anything happen to them.”

Mia crosses her arms over her chest and sticks

out a hip. "Really? Then what do you call this? They redecorated her home because of you. What will they do if they find her?" Mia stares at me. "Is this from that guy who came to visit?" She clicks her fingers, trying to remember his name. "Hunter? Right? His name was Hunter."

"Yes, he was part of the crew I used to run with."

"I'm guessing the crew who double-crossed you and put you in jail?" she asks Renny.

"Mia, this isn't our business," states Tyrone.

Mia looks up at her younger brother. "She's our *friend*, Tyrone. It makes it *our* business."

Reaching out, I place a hand on Mia's upper arm. "It's why I left. They threatened me and Zachary. Renny took us in. We're safe, I promise."

"How? It sounds like it's just the three of you. And you said crew, meaning more than one person. Can he protect you on his own?"

"I'm safer in a small town where strangers stick out than I am here in the city where everyone is a stranger."

Mia sucks in a breath and studies my face. "You have a point."

Smiling, I put an arm around her. "You can come visit as soon as we have our own place."

"And after we clean up this mess," Mia states flatly.

"That's the spirit," I say loudly and a little too cheerfully.

Renny raises his eyebrows and goes back to sweeping.

CHAPTER 19

RENNY

Mia's words swirl around in my head. *'Can he protect you on his own?'* The truth is, until Sergio moves against my old friends, I can't. There's safety in numbers, and if I join the Savage Angels MC, we will all be safe. From what I've seen, Dane doesn't let anyone mess with those in his club. He takes care of them. Sure, he rules with an iron fist, but since he's become a husband and family man, he's tried to steer the MC out of illegal activities, which is something that appeals to me.

"Penny for your thoughts?" asks Thea as she places a plate in front of me.

"Sorry, babe. I'm glad I was with you today."

"Apart from my couch, coffee table, vase, and pillows, nothing else was broken. I got lucky."

Even after tidying the wreckage, Thea focuses on

the positive. She simply boxes up the belongings worth keeping and moves on with a smile. She and Zach never had much, only each other. And now, most importantly, they have me.

"I kinda whipped up a stew from the freezer," she calls over her shoulder, tending the stove. "Not too many veggies, though… only some canned corn. It's mostly meat…" she pauses, glancing my way, "… and rice."

"Sounds perfect," I assure her. "Meat and rice is a classic combo."

I don't want Thea feeling bad about a simple meal. If she only knew that after years of bland prison chow, anything homemade tastes like a five-star dinner. For tonight, the company matters more than the food. Her effort and care in preparing it are enough to make this stew special.

After everything we faced today, having a quiet dinner together feels like the calm after the storm. Thea's optimism never ceases to lift my spirits. With her by my side, any hardship feels manageable.

We eat in silence, music playing in the background. It's a comfortable silence. Thea hums along to the song while she eats, and it makes me smile. She catches me staring at her and stops.

"What?"

"This… it's nice." I reach across the table and grab her hand. "You and me, sharing a meal. All that's missing is Zach."

"I should ring Destiny... make sure he's okay."

"Is it okay if I have a shower?"

Thea stands, opens a box, and hands me a towel, "Of course. I've left soap in the shower, so you're good to go."

I take the proffered towel with a nod and enter the bathroom. Inside, I switch on the shower—it's one of those tub showers with a curtain. As the water warms up, I step in, letting it cascade over my tired muscles. The soap has a crisp, clean fragrance, but her shampoo makes me smile—the fruity blend I've come to associate with Thea. The smell envelops me in thoughts of her, washing away the day's stress.

When I'm done, I dry myself and drape the towel around my hips, securing it at the waist. My bag is in Thea's room, so I open the bathroom door and pad into her room. Thea is standing there, staring off into space.

"Hey, bathroom's free."

Turning around, Thea gasps softly as her gaze meets mine. She steps closer, her hand coming to rest on my bare chest. I shiver as her fingers gently trace over my tattoos, her touch igniting my skin. "So many," she whispers, studying the intricate designs.

I cover her hand with mine, holding it over my heart. Thea's eyes lift to lock with mine, luminous and full of longing. Unable to resist any longer, I draw her body against me.

Her lips part in anticipation as I cradle her cheek, our faces inches apart. The tension thrums between us. When our mouths finally meet, the kiss deepens instantly. All the desire we've been holding back explodes in passion.

My hands tangle in her hair as our lips crash together, claiming each other hungrily. She clings to me, molded against my frame. We come up breathless, foreheads touching, still wrapped in each other's embrace. No more waiting, no more holding back. This kiss has sparked an inferno, and I never want the flames between us to be extinguished.

The towel falls from my hips, exposing my hard cock. Desperate to feel every inch of her, my fingers hook the bottom of her shirt, and I drag it up and over her head. Falling to my knees, I undo her jeans and pull them and her panties down her legs. Thea steps out of them, and I stare up at her, eager to imprint her beautiful body to my memory.

She's right. Her body has changed—it's fuller and bears the marks of our child she carried. This body is nothing short of amazing.

Splaying a hand on her stomach, I whisper, "Perfect."

Thea shakes her head. "You're... you're not disappointed?"

Standing, I press my lips to hers. My tongue presses past the seam of her lips, desperate to taste her. My arms encircle her slim frame, her supple body against my muscular chest. Thea melts into me, her fingers splayed across my back. Fervently, I kiss her, unable to get enough of her, cradling her face as I deepen the kiss, expressing much of my pent-up longing.

Thea sighs as my hands begin to roam, caressing her hips and back. She arches into me wantonly, responding to my touch. Our kisses turn hungry, almost frantic, as our passion mounts. Laying her down on the bed, my thigh slips between her legs, my arousal evident against her abdomen.

Pressed together, our hands roam, my heart races, and Thea's fingers grip my head, trying to pull me closer. My lips trail down her neck as she throws her head back, eyes closed. In this moment, nothing else exists but us. The world falls away as I lose myself in her body.

Thea opens her legs wider, and slowly, my cock enters her. She cries out, her fingers digging into my back. With a grunt, I pull out, thrust back inside her, and Thea whispers my name.

"Renny." It sounds like a purr and spurs me on.

Thrusting faster, Thea matches my pace, and I feel the first shudder of her orgasm. I place a finger over her nub, pressing down, and her pussy contracts around my dick. For years, I dreamed about this, and in all my thoughts, it was always Thea, but this is more than I dared hope for.

Burying myself inside her as far as I can go, I reach my orgasm with a mighty roar, my seed spilling into Thea. Slowly, I move in and out of her, enjoying the feel of the aftershocks of her pussy as she takes all I have to give.

When I'm done, I pull out and collapse beside her. One of Thea's hands rests on my chest, the only sounds are our labored breaths.

"I'm so sorry," I whisper.

Thea turns and rests on one of her arms. "What for?"

"It was a little... quick."

Thea kisses my lips and shakes her head. "It was perfect."

Chuckling, I drag her up my body. "Next time will be better."

"I'm not sure it could get much better."

"Practice makes perfect."

She rests her hands on my chest, then puts her chin on them. "I think I like the sound of that."

I wrap a tendril of her hair around one of my fingers, and nervously ask, "Was it good for you?"

Her mouth opens slightly, and she appears surprised. "Couldn't you tell? Couldn't you feel..." her words trail off.

Moving quickly, I flip us over so I'm on top. "I could feel. I guess it's been a long time, and I needed to hear the words."

"I told you, Renny, it was *perfect.*"

With a smirk, I ask, "Want to take a shower with me?"

Thea grins. "Absolutely."

CHAPTER 20

THEA

Never have I slept so soundly or content. The sun's early morning rays filter through my floral curtains, and Renny has me tucked into his side. He's snoring a little, his breaths sounding deep and totally relaxed.

His very touch ignited a fire within me, and from the way he responded to me, I guess he feels the same. Renny's body is totally different from the man I once knew. He has muscles where I didn't know you could have muscles, and there's not an ounce of fat on him.

Though passionate utterances were exchanged in the throes of lovemaking last night, the words playing over in my mind are his admission, *'It's always been you.'*

It could mean anything, but I'm hopeful it means

he wants more than a night of passion or a casual encounter.

Renny stirs, his arms going over his head, and he stretches. “Good morning.”

“Good morning.”

“How long have you been awake?”

He moves and lies on top of me, kissing my lips.

“No!” I shriek.

Renny rears back. “What?”

“Morning breath!” I push him off me and hurry to the bathroom.

While I’m brushing my teeth, Renny leans against the doorway, naked, with a grin on his face.

“You know I’ve got morning breath too.”

I spit the foam into the sink and wipe my face with a towel. “I know, but I’m not worried about you. I’m worried about me.”

Renny frowns. “Makes no sense, woman. Now you have fresh, minty breath, and I have something that smells like the bottom of a parrot’s cage.”

“I don’t care.”

Renny brushes past me to freshen up in the bathroom while I hurry back to the bedroom, attempting to pose alluringly on the bed, though it proves challenging with my unruly hair sticking out at odd angles. I try desperately to smooth down the flyaway strands before he returns and catches me looking disheveled. Despite my best efforts, I cannot seem to tame my wild mane or arrange myself elegantly. I can only hope he finds my messy morning-after look charming rather than comical.

Renny saunters into the room, standing at the end of the bed, cock at attention. "You are beautiful."

Self-consciously, I pat my hair. "Really?"

Renny presses his lips together, quirking them to one side. "Absolutely," he affirms, prowls up the bed, and tugs the sheet down my body. "Let me show you how much."

His eyes blaze with passion, and speech fails me. But my body intuitively understands how to respond to his touch. Renny's mouth captures my nipple, sucking and biting until it pebbles under his touch, first one, then the other.

Renny presses his lips to my ear. "Do you want more?"

"Yes," I purr.

He sucks on my neck, and it feels so good that I arch against him. Renny drags his teeth down my body, and I shudder with excitement. He always knew how to get my body to respond.

Damn, Renny is good at this.

His hands explore every inch of me. Pushing my breasts together, he rests his face between them and then inhales, rubbing the scruff of his jaw over them. I gasp at the sensation and buck against him.

Renny positions his cock at my entrance, but I want more. With a grunt, I flip us and maneuver his shaft between my legs, then slowly ease down on top of him. His eyes roll back in his head. Not wanting to rush this, I keep my pace slow and steady as I move up and down. His hands dig into my waist as he tries to move me faster. Closing my eyes, I concentrate on chasing that thread of passion only Renny has ever discovered. My body is tense as the pressure builds, and Renny matches me with every stroke.

"*Fuck, Thea.*" My eyes open, and he's gritting his teeth as he thrusts into me. "You're so fucking beautiful."

Gripping the back of his head, I feel my orgasm building as I increase my pace. Renny rocks up into me harder, and I know he's barely hanging on. The first wave of ecstasy pulses through my body, and I cry out his name.

Renny moves me faster, diving in deeper as wave after wave rocks through me. The feel of his cock inside me consumes me as I move mindlessly, drawing out my orgasm. Then with a grunt, he stops moving, smiles at me, pulls back slightly, then rams into me again with a low growl of satisfaction.

Spent, I fall onto him, and he wraps his arms around me, holding me close.

There's no way I'm letting Renny go now.

This feeling of wholeness washes over me, and I know he's the one for me.

He's always been my destiny.

CHAPTER 21

RENNY

Thea and I sit on the couch in Destiny and Kade's home. Her meager possessions are neatly stacked in the bedroom upstairs. We steal kisses and relish this time alone, fingers intertwined. In some ways, it feels like no time has passed, yet Thea's mention of events and shows I've missed remind me how much we still need to learn about each other.

Prison stops time.

The routine stays the same as the days blur together. I spent most days pumping iron, quickly realizing I needed to be able to defend myself. More than one inmate tried to test me, but by the grace of God, I overcame them all.

"What was it like?"

I'm tracing patterns on Thea's neck.

"What was what like?"

"Prison."

Sucking in a breath, I let it out slowly. "It was the same mundane stuff every day. Like watching the same episode of your favorite TV show, except it wasn't fun. There are politics in prison, and whether you want to or not, you have to pick a side. The guards are the worst..." he pauses for a moment, then continues, "... pay them enough, and they'll turn a blind eye. Piss them off, and they'll make you suffer."

"How did you survive?"

"Brute strength, and there's safety in numbers. I became friends with the right people."

The front door opens, and Zach comes running into the living room.

Thea moves away from me and gets up to greet him. "Hey, honey, did you miss me?"

"It was one night, Mom."

"I missed you."

He grins and nods. "Yeah, I missed you."

Thea wraps him in a hug, and he rolls his eyes at me over her shoulder.

"Hey, bud. Where's your Aunty Destiny?"

"She said to tell you she's working late, and Dane wants to see you."

"Dane? The biker?" asks Thea.

"Yep, my boss."

She nods. "Did you tell him you were taking off?"

"I did, but they're shorthanded at the garage, so

he probably wants to make sure I'm coming in tomorrow. I might leave you two to catch up and go see what he wants."

Thea stares down at Zach. "Want to help me make dinner?"

He looks a little sheepish. "Ahh… I told Aunty Destiny you make the best fried chicken and mashed potatoes, so she got all the ingredients."

"Did you now?" Thea laughs. "Well, I guess that's what we're having. Do you want to get the chicken out of the fridge?"

"Yes, ma'am."

Zach walks toward the kitchen, and I stand, kissing Thea lightly on the lips.

"Are you going to tell him about us?"

She shakes her head. "Not yet. It's been him and me for so long, and I don't want him to get his hopes up if..."

I kiss her again. "I get it. It's okay. We'll take this slow. I'm not going anywhere."

"Thank you."

I kiss her nose and say, "I'll be back within the hour."

Thea smiles, and it brightens her whole face. "I'll get dinner ready."

"I can't wait to taste the *best* fried chicken."

"Our son might exaggerate a little." She holds up her hands and spreads them wide.

"That much, huh?"

"I guess you're going to find out."

The door to the garage office is open. I stick my head in, and a tall, attractive brunette glances up from the desk with a smile.

"Hello, how can I help you?"

"I'm Renny. I work here."

She stands, extending a slender hand. "I'm Addy. I handle the paperwork, and I'm Jonas' partner."

I shake her hand. Smooth skin, firm grip. "He's mentioned you and that you own the motel in town."

"That's me." She shuffles papers on the desk and holds out a sheet. "You need to fill this out. I know they've paid cash, but it'll be easier if you open an account."

I take the form, glancing over the bank details. "Will do. Have you seen Dane?"

"He's in the clubhouse."

"Thanks." I wave the paper. "I'll get this back soon."

Addy smiles, brushing a strand of chestnut hair behind her ear. "Please do. And if you see Jonas, tell him to get over here. I can barely read his chicken scratch."

I grin and nod, then head out across the compound. Loud voices echo from the clubhouse. As I step onto the stairs, a body comes flying out the doors, hitting the dirt with a heavy thud.

He rolls to his side, wheezing and winded.

Dane thunders out after him, looming above. "Fix your fucking attitude, Reb. I won't put up with your shit." He jabs a finger at the man. "Ever since Ruby came here, you've been insufferable. No one's stealing your woman. Sure, we appreciate her art, but we all know she's yours. So, stop being a dick."

Rebel looks visibly shaken as he lies in the dirt.

Dane turns to me, demeanor shifting. "Renny, good you're back. There's a Corvette needing a serious rebuild. Owner says cost is no object."

His sudden casual tone is jarring after the violence. He helps Rebel to his feet, his pride clearly wounded as he limps away.

Dane sighs, scrubbing his bearded face. "Women, more trouble than they're worth some days."

I raise an eyebrow. "How's Kat?"

He barks a laugh. "Good, thanks for looking after her the other night. She likes Thea."

I nod. "You wanted to see me?"

"Yeah, let's chat." He waves me into the clubhouse.

Dane strides back inside, letting out a sharp whistle as he circles his hand in the air. A few guys rise and follow us into the meeting room. Dane takes the head seat while the others settle into familiar positions. I hesitate before sitting, aware this room is reserved for formal club meetings and 'church.' As a non-member, my presence is unusual. The best chair is at the other end of the table, so I pull it out and sit.

Dane holds a hand to his chest. "I'm the president of this chapter, and in case you didn't know…" he points at the man to his left, "… this is Jonas, our VP. To my right is Dirt, he's my sergeant at arms. Next is Bear, he's our road captain, and across from him is Keg. We are obviously all patched-in members of the MC."

The men wave or give chin lifts, and I dip my head in return.

"I'm grateful for the work. Thank you for giving me a job."

Dane rocks back, his hulking frame threatening to break the seat. "You do good work. There's been no complaints from the customers or the other brothers." His eyes flick to Jonas, who nods. "We know it's difficult settling back into regular life after a stint. But you seem to be doing well, Renny. I know we've talked about it, but we'd like you to join us. You'd only be a prospect, but in time, you'll become a patched-in member."

"Providing you make the cut," says Keg.

Dane stares at Keg for a beat, then stares back at

me. "What do you say?"

"I didn't do what they put me in prison for."

Dane taps the table. "We don't care about that."

Holding up a hand, I say, "But there's plenty of shit I did do before I got put away. Some of that shit is still following me around. My concern is it will blow back on the club, and I don't want anyone else hurt."

Dane's brow furrows. "Anything you say in this room stays in this room. Care to share?"

"The men who put me in prison are on the shit list for Sergio Alvarez."

"The Juarez Cartel?" Dirt questions incredulously. "Sergio Alvarez himself?"

I nod. "One and the same. We're friends... in a manner of speaking."

Dirt shakes his head, eyebrows raised. "The man's a killer. I doubt he has any *real* friends."

I chuckle darkly. "Save his life, and he'll like you plenty."

Dane holds up a hand. "Start from the beginning. Why's he after the ones who locked you up?"

I suck in a breath. "Because I told him they stole his money."

Dirt barks a laugh. "I've heard about the Juarez Cartel getting ripped off for millions, but no one was ever caught. What made him believe you when you fingered these guys?"

I meet his gaze steadily. "Because I was the one

who took it. They helped me, then double-crossed me. Sheer luck, Sergio and I got thrown together inside. He trusts me and has no reason to doubt me. And when he finds the cash stashed in one of their houses, they're as good as dead."

Dirt tilts his head to the side and stares down at the table. "How do you know they won't give you up?"

"Sergio isn't known for asking too many questions. Once he has the money, he'll eliminate them."

Dane's lips come together in a pressed line. "You're playing a deadly game."

"I know. I promised Thea I wouldn't fall back into old habits. Killing them would tarnish my promise, but by using Sergio, my hands are clean."

"Hardly," interjects Jonas.

"I'm only telling you as you deserve to know what you're getting. There's safety in numbers. Sergio hasn't moved against them yet, and they're waiting for me to attack. They could get nervous and strike first. I'm not worried for me, but I am for Destiny, Kade, Thea, and my son."

Dirt opens his mouth to speak, but Dane stands, cutting him off. "How well do you know Sergio?"

"Well enough."

His eyes bore into mine as he studies me. "If you still want in, we'll have you."

"And if it all blows up in my face?"

"We'll protect the people around you, but you will be on your own."

Dane moves and opens a drawer behind him, pulling out a cut. "Loyalty to the club comes first, above all else. The club is your family now. Respect the hierarchy and club officers... you'll meet them all in due course. Follow the president's orders... I will *not* be disobeyed. Attend all club meetings and events. Don't discuss club business with outsiders. What happens in the club stays there. Defend and protect your brothers when needed. Have their back. Don't covet another member's property or woman. Respect each other. Wear your colors proudly, keep them safeguarded, and treat them with respect. Represent the club well. Act with honor and integrity according to our code. Brotherhood above all. These are our rules. Judge sponsored you, so he's the one you need to see if you have any questions, but we're all here to help." He moves around the table toward me, holding out the cut. "Welcome to the family."

I take the denim cut from him and put it on. Dane smiles and slaps me on the back, his heavy hand rattling my bones in brotherly affection. The others stand, some offer handshakes, and others, like Dane, pound on my back or arm.

"Thank you."

"No matter what happens, you're one of us now," says Dirt.

Smiling, I hold out a hand to him. "Almost. I'm guessing as a prospect, I get the shit detail?"

Bear laughs. "Yep, and your first act as a prospect is to get your butt into Dane's garage this weekend. It's the large building near his house. There's a basket case you can do up as your own until you get a proper bike."

"Basket case?"

"It's what we call a bike that has been in an accident and can't be repaired. We strip them down and recreate them," says Jonas.

"Zeke mentioned Frankenstein's."

"Yep, that's them, but the difference is this Frankenstein will be yours." Bear opens the door to the room. "See you bright and early Saturday morning."

CHAPTER 22

THEA

Things are finally coming together. I have my job at the café, enrolled Zachary in the local school, and Renny and I have a bond that feels stronger than ever. The only missing piece is a place of our own. After my shift today, I'm going to check out a small two-bedroom apartment just off Main Street. The owner is a regular at the café and said the place is mine if I want it.

I finish the breakfast rush. Bid farewell to my favorite customers and Howie as the new girl starts her shift at two o'clock. The air still holds the warmth of summer as I make my way down the tree-lined street. People smile and wave when they recognize me from the diner, welcoming me into the fabric of this little town.

I find the address easily. It's a well-kept red brick

building. Inside, the owner, Gus, greets me enthusiastically. He's an elderly gentleman, stooped from years of hard work, but his eyes twinkle kindly behind thick glasses. I instantly feel at ease with him as he shows me around the cozy apartment. It's perfect—small rooms but filled with light. The kitchen is a decent size, and the living area has enough space for a couch, television, and maybe, in the near future, a game station for Zachary.

As I chat with the owner and fill out paperwork to make the apartment officially mine, I feel a sense of hope bloom in my chest. This is exactly the fresh start Zachary and I need. And maybe, just maybe, it could become Renny's home too.

Gus takes the paperwork off me. "I'll need to check your references. It shouldn't take but a day or two."

"Thank you so much."

Gus looks around. "If you need any maintenance done, give me a call. The last tenant complained about the hot water, but it works fine."

"Why'd they complain?"

Gus laughs. "She kept running out of hot water, but I think that happens if you take really long showers."

"Ahh… gotcha. I'm an in-and-out kinda girl."

Gus taps the side of his nose. "I knew you'd get it."

He walks me out, and I stroll the rest of the way alone back to Destiny's. No one is home, so I step upstairs, shower, and then come back down to make dinner for everyone.

I've got the music blaring as I chop up vegetables and dance around the kitchen. It's not until I hear a chuckle that I stop. Kade is there, arms crossed, hair over one eye, grinning at me.

"Nice moves."

"Shut up." I wave the knife at him. "Are there any veggies you don't like?"

"All of them."

"I'm serious."

"So am I."

"Kade, you've eaten everything I've put in front of you."

"I have. You're a good cook, but if I could have meat with a side of meat, I'd be a happy man." He moves closer and inspects what I've done so far. "What are we having?"

"Destiny said she likes Chinese, so I thought I'd do a stir-fry, which means veggies and meat."

"Could you do more meat for me and less vegetables?"

With a nod, I say, "I can try."

Kade grins. "Where's the prospect?"

"Who?"

"The prospect, Renny."

Confused at the word, I shake my head. "Why are

you calling him that?"

Kade strokes his chin, looking confused. "Didn't he tell you he's a prospect in the MC? Dane asked him to join a week ago."

"What?"

"Yeah. He has a year to prove himself, and so long as he follows the rules, he'll get patched in. Everyone seems to like him, and he's a hard worker, so I can't see Renny having any difficulties."

My mouth goes dry.

Renny never told me.

No more secrets?

He knew I'd disapprove of him joining an MC.

Dammit! He hasn't changed at all.

I thought we were building a life together, a foundation to build on, and he's running with a gang. It's the same old shit, only this time we have a son, one I won't subject to club life and their initiations. No way is any child of mine going to end up in prison or worse.

My hands clench into fists, nails biting into my palms. Frustration and disappointment roil in my gut like a storm. I thought I could trust Renny and believed he had matured during his time away. But now I see the good man I fell in love with so long ago is still trapped beneath layers of criminal habits. Habits I won't expose Zachary to, no matter what it takes.

Kade studies me, waiting for an answer. "Is

everything okay?" he finally asks.

I force a smile across my face. "Of course. Maybe Renny was waiting for the right time to tell me?" But my gut twists with unease.

Zachary bounds through the house, bookbag dangling from his arm. "Hey, Mom, what's for dinner?"

"Chicken stir-fry."

"With crispy noodles?" he asks hopefully.

"You know it."

Zachary does a little victory dance which makes Kade chuckle.

Renny and I are going to have a serious talk tonight.

"Honey, do your homework, wash up, then come set the table."

"Okay, Mom."

Zachary and Kade perform some elaborate handshake before he scampers upstairs.

"Don't run!" I yell at the ceiling.

Kade leans on the counter beside me. "Why didn't Renny tell you?"

Damn, he's perceptive. With a shake of my head, I brush it off. "Do you have onion powder?"

"No clue. I'll check the spice rack."

After a minute, he produces the small jar triumphantly. "Aha, got it!"

"You're a lifesaver." I force another smile, ignoring the unease churning within me.

Kade leaves me to my thoughts as I continue cooking, remembering all the broken promises from Renny's past. My guard had finally lowered over time, but now feels the need to reinforce those around my heart.

It is late when Renny comes for a visit. I am sitting alone on the front steps, staring at the vast expanse of stars glittering brightly against the dark night sky. The house behind me is quiet—Zachary is tucked into bed, the dinner dishes have been cleaned and put away, and Destiny is in her study working. I'm not sure where Kade is, maybe with the rest of his MC.

I hear Renny's footsteps approach before I see him. "Hey, babe, what are you doing sitting out here by yourself?" he asks. I turned to look at him, his handsome face faintly illuminated by the porch light.

"You lied to me," I reply bluntly.

Renny's brows furrow in confusion. "Come again?"

"Were you ever going to tell me you joined the Savage Angels?" I question, trying to keep the hurt out of my voice.

Renny sighs deeply and runs both hands through the stubble on his head before sitting down on the step beside me. "I was going to tell you, I swear. They're having a party next week. I wanted you to meet the guys before I said anything about joining."

Shaking my head, I'm unconvinced by his excuses. "So, you lied to me this whole time?"

"I didn't lie exactly... I just didn't mention it yet," Renny explains.

"Not telling me is the same as lying," I say as anger wells inside me. "I thought we didn't keep secrets from each other."

Renny reaches for my hand, but I pull away, the feeling of betrayal sitting heavily in my chest. I look back at the indifferent stars and feel as cold as they are.

"They aren't what you think."

"They aren't criminals? They don't break the law?" Standing, I throw my hands in the air. "You haven't changed at all, have you? You're exactly the same, but instead of childhood friends you can't see the truth about, you're replacing them with these bikers and once again putting me in danger."

"Thea, please—" Renny starts, holding up his hands defensively.

"No!" I cut him off sharply. "Don't try to talk your way out of this, Renny, because it's not just me anymore." I lower my voice. "We have a son now."

Renny's face falls at my words. "There are things you don't know."

Disgusted, I turn my back on him and grab the doorknob. "There always is with you," I mutter bitterly before stepping inside and shutting the door firmly between us. My heart aches with anger and disappointment as I lean against the closed door.

I thought Renny had grown up, but some things never change.

The next morning, I wait until Destiny and Kade leave the house, then I pack up the belongings I came to town with. Zachary's face goes from happiness to sadness when he sees what I'm doing.

"I don't want to go."

"I know, and I don't want to either."

"Then please, Mom, let's stay," he pleads.

Sitting on the edge of the bed, I grasp his small hands in mine. "It's my job as your mom to always take care of you. I know you're not going to understand this right now, but that's what I'm doing."

"I like it here. My dad is here, and I made a friend

at school. Please, Mom, can't we stay?"

A tear runs down his face, and my throat constricts at the sight of it.

"You can call your dad when we get home. We're going back to Mia and your old school."

Zachary nods and complies, but I know he's hurting. For once, he had a family, a father, and right now, he doesn't understand, but I can't let him fall prey to the evils of Renny's poor choices.

Picking up my battered suitcase with Zachary's hand in mine, I lead us out of the house and to the bus stop on Main Street. We get there as the bus pulls up. The bus driver puts our suitcase in the hold, and we board the bus. I look around the small town I've grown to love and push Zachary ahead of me up the steps. My eyes land on Dane, the president of the Savage Angels, and I can't help the feeling of anger flooding my system. He raises a hand to wave at me but stops halfway. No doubt my face conveys my feelings in this moment.

I board the bus, let Zachary have a window seat, and send a silent prayer to the gods, hoping he'll forgive me one day.

CHAPTER 23

RENNY

My gut twists with guilt as I think about my conversation with Thea last night. She's right. I should have been honest and told her about joining the Savage Angels and why I did it. I can't blame her for being angry with me. We're still getting to know each other and building trust.

My cell phone rings, and the caller ID flashes. 'President.'

"Hey, Prez, I'm on my way," I answer.

"To where?" Dane asks gruffly.

"Work," I reply, confused.

"Renny..." Dane says with a sigh, "... did you know Thea and Zach were getting on the bus this morning?"

I feel my stomach drop. "No. He has school, and she has work at the café."

"Well, she had a suitcase with her. And I called into Betty's. Howie said Thea phoned yesterday and quit her job," Dane informs me.

My pulse quickens with panic.

She's leaving town?

And taking Zachary with her?

I rack my brain, trying to figure out where she would go. Have I ruined everything between us for good?

"Has the bus left?"

"Yeah. I thought things were good between you both?"

"I fucked up, and we had an argument last night."

Dane makes a clicking sound. "Maybe let her go? Let her simmer down. It's a long bus trip back to where she came from. By the time she gets there, she might see things differently."

Everything inside me screams no, but why would she run? Last night, she said I hadn't changed. Well, maybe she hasn't either? If Thea runs at the first sign of trouble, perhaps she isn't the woman I need her to be.

"Renny?"

"Yeah, Prez?"

"You can take off after her. Take all the time you need."

"No, you're right. I'll give her some space. Who knows, maybe it will do us both some good."

"Okay, brother. If you need anything, you

call. Yeah?"

"Thanks, Dane, and I appreciate the heads-up."

He ends the call, and I drive to Destiny's home. Opening the front door, I take the stairs two at a time and walk down the hallway to their room. The bed is made, and there are two handwritten notes on the bed. One is for Destiny, and the other is for me. I don't touch Destiny's, but I pick up mine and open it.

Renny,

Zachary deserves better than an absent, reckless father. I can't trust you not to bring danger into our home. Who knows what trouble the MC will drag you into that could hurt you or us?

If you quit the MC for good, then maybe there's a shot for us in the future. My priority is protecting Zachary. It always has been.

You were the one who said no secrets, *and you broke your own rule. How am I supposed to trust you?*

I'll call when we are settled in our old apartment.

Always yours,
Thea

Letting go of the paper, it flutters back to the bed. I stare at it and shake my head. If I'd told Thea why I joined the MC, would it have made a difference?

Destiny bursts into the room, gaze darting around frantically. "Are they gone?"

"Yes."

"Why? What happened? Did you two have a fight?" she fires questions at me.

I point at my cut. "She didn't approve of the MC. She's worried I'm falling back into old habits."

Destiny shakes her head. "But she knows Kade and met Zeke. How can she think they're bad?"

"It's my fault. I didn't tell her… I kept my joining from her."

"Why did you join?"

"Brotherhood and trouble might be coming for me. Dane said he'd protect you, Thea, and Zach. I did it for all of you."

Destiny puts a hand on her hip. "Men!" She moves closer and shoves me. "In case you didn't know this, Renny, we are capable of taking care of ourselves. What did you think we were doing for the past eight years?"

"You have Kade."

"And before Kade, I had *me*. Me who was violated

because of a threat to you. Me who picked herself up and made something of herself! *Me*, Renny. I've been looking after myself for a long time, and so has Thea." Her words spew out of her mouth like gasoline on fire.

"You were violated because of me?"

Destiny's face pales. She shakes her head, holds up a hand, and her eyes drop to my chest. "It wasn't on you." Her eyes come back to me. "But this, Thea and Zach, that is on you. *Fix it*." Destiny turns and strides for the door.

"I don't understand, Destiny. What wasn't on me?"

Kade appears in the doorway, his eyes on her.

"One day, I'll tell you, but right now, you need to get our family back." Destiny puts her hand on Kade's chest as she passes him and continues down the hallway.

"Kade, what did she mean?"

He sucks in a breath. "Told you when we first met, it's not my place to tell you. I heard what she said, but she was angry. She didn't mean it. She knows it wasn't your fault. I will tell you, the man who violated her can't hurt anyone else."

"Thea and Zach are gone."

Kade's lips go down in the corners. "That is on me. I told her you'd joined the MC. I didn't know it was a secret."

With a sigh, I rub the back of my head. "I was

going to tell her at the party. I thought if she got to know the MC and met some of the brothers and their women, she might see them differently. Why is she against the MC?"

"She isn't, not really. Thea thinks I'm falling back into old habits."

"Because of your past?" I nod in agreement. "So, prove her wrong."

I belt out a laugh. "And how do I do that?"

"Go get her. Tell her why you did what you did."

"It's a three-day journey for her and Zach."

"All the more reason to find her on the trail."

"Dane thinks I should give her time to think."

Kade shrugs. "In my short, unremarkable life, I have to tell you, I think it's a mistake."

"Unremarkable?"

Kade smirks. "Well, it was until I met your sister. And, Renny? If she were mad at me, I'd tie her to a chair if it meant I could keep her."

"Man, that's creepy."

Kade chuckles. "You know what I mean."

Kade walks out of the room, and I pull out my cell to call Thea. It goes straight to voicemail.

I listen to her voice message and then say, "There are things you don't know. I was going to tell you. But you're right, by not telling you, it's a—"

Beep.

"Shit!" I redial her number and listen to her message all over again. "Thea, I'm sorry. That's the short of it. I'll come get you both if you want."

Beep.

In frustration, I throw my phone on the floor and then immediately scramble to pick it up.

Thankfully, it's not broken.

I guess all I can do now is wait.

CHAPTER 24

THEA

The message Renny left on my phone sounds genuine, but he did lie, and I need time away from him to clear my thoughts. By the time we make the long journey back to a waiting Mia at the train station, I've decided I made the right decision. If he'd really cared, surely he would have come after us?

"Hey, you two!" Mia cries as she hugs Zachary, then me.

"Hey, Mia," Zachary replies without an ounce of enthusiasm.

She stares at me, and I shrug. "We're tired. It's been a long few days."

"Well, let's get you home." Mia links her arm through mine. "I'm thinking homemade waffles, maple syrup, and whipped cream will fix what ails you."

Zachary smiles at her, the first one I've seen since we left Tourmaline. "Yes, ma'am."

Together, we walk to Mia's beat-up white Honda, and she drives us back to our old apartment building.

"Has he rented our apartment yet?"

"Not yet. He's had a couple of people through, but I make sure to vet them first. So far, no one seems good enough to live next door to me."

"Mia, what did you do?"

"Music or I scream about the devil or pretend I can see ghosts in the hallway."

Laughing, I say, "You do not." She smirks. "You don't really, do you?"

"Nah." Mia shakes her head, and we walk up the stairs. "But the only one he's had through was a little old lady who looked like she was going to kick it the minute she walked up the stairs."

"I know how she feels."

Zachary bounds up the stairs, and when we make it to the third floor, he's standing outside Mia's door.

"Tyrone is inside. Knock, and he'll let you in," Mia calls from the top of the stairs.

Zachary raps his knuckles loudly on the wooden door, it opens, and he disappears inside.

"Thanks for this, Mia."

"What happened? I thought you'd found a new

life and left us all behind."

"So did I."

"Okay, let's get Zachary and Tyrone fed, then you and I can sit, drink, and you can tell me all about it."

"I feel like death and probably smell like it too. Do you think we could just eat, have a shower, and in the morning, I'll fill you in?"

Mia shrugs a shoulder up to one ear. "Or we could do that."

Laughing, we enter her apartment.

"Okay, let me get this straight... he joined an MC? How does that make any sense?"

"I know, right? Worst of all, he lied."

Mia sips her coffee. "Girrrlll, I knew he was trouble the minute I laid eyes on him."

"I wish I'd figured it out earlier."

Mia nods sagely and then frowns. "But I have to say, I haven't seen you that happy in a long time."

Her words bring tears to my eyes. Not wanting them to fall, I swallow rapidly and shake my head.

"D-do you think they'll let me have my apartment back?"

"Technically, it's still yours. You paid the back

rent plus two weeks."

"Renny did that."

"Who cares? Ring the landlord and ask. The worst he can say is no. You and Zachary are welcome to stay here as long as you need."

Mia puts an arm around me, and I lean into her. I'm so grateful to have her in my life.

"Thanks, honey."

"Pfft! It's what we do. I'm here for you, and you're here for me. Men come and go, but we'll always be friends."

If I'd known then what was about to happen, I would never have come back to my old apartment.

I would have stayed in Tourmaline.

CHAPTER 25

RENNY

It's been a week since Thea and Zachary left, and the pain is unbearable. I've sent her countless messages begging her to respond, but nothing. Being separated from them is torture. Zach probably thinks I don't care, or maybe I even wanted them to leave. The not knowing eats away at my soul.

Work is my only escape. I go in at dawn and leave after sunset to avoid going home to an empty cabin. On the way, I stop by Dane's or have dinner with Destiny and Kade. The nights alone are the worst, as my every thought revolves around Thea and Zachary.

Late afternoon, my phone rings. The caller ID says it's Thea. I scramble out from under the car and anxiously answer.

"Thea?" I ask hopefully.

"Dad?" Zach's voice answers me.

"Zach! Bud, it's so good to hear your voice."

A sob escapes him. "Dad, we need you."

My heart drops. "Calm down. What happened?"

"Mia got hurt. We're at the hospital. Mom doesn't know I called." He sniffles.

I sprint down Main Street toward Destiny's office. "What happened, Zach?"

"A man tried to hurt Mom, but Mia got in the way. We were outside our apartment. There was so much blood. We're at the hospital waiting to see if Mia is going to be okay. I'm in the waiting room. Mom went to get coffee. It's okay I called, isn't it?" His voice sounds so unsure, as though he's doing something wrong.

"What hospital are you at?" I burst into the law offices where Destiny works. "And, of course, it's okay. Zach, you did the right thing."

The receptionist's expression shifts to one of alarm, and she hastily points down the hallway toward Destiny's office. I rap my knuckles on the door then open it. She's sitting behind her desk and stares up at me sharply.

"We're at the Mercy Hospital."

"Mercy Hospital, right. Was your mom hurt?"

Destiny stands.

"No, Dad. Only Mia."

"I'm coming. You take care of your mom until I

get there, and you call me if you need anything. Got it?"

"Yes, sir."

I end the call and stare at my sister.

"Are they okay?"

"Someone went after Thea. Her friend, Mia, got hurt, and it sounds bad. Destiny, I need to borrow your truck."

"It's a day's drive to get there. Let me call Kade."

"How can Kade help?"

Destiny picks up her phone. "Honey, you're in the Savage Angels now. They're one of the largest MCs in the US. There's not much they can't do."

A trip that would normally take me twenty-four hours took me nineteen. I park in the hospital parking lot and jog into the hospital. It's midmorning when I enter the lobby. A large woman sits behind a glass partition, arguing with a man who thumps the glass before storming off. Her annoyed gaze lands on me.

"Can I help you?" she asks flatly.

"They brought a friend of mine in yesterday," I explain urgently.

"What's your friend's name?"

I hesitate as I only know Mia's first name. "Mia."

The woman looks at me hopefully. "Mia?"

"I don't know her last name. My son called, saying she'd been attacked on the street. There was a lot of blood."

"Sir, I need a last name to help you."

I hold up a finger and dial Thea again, but it goes straight to voicemail—same as every other time I've tried calling since Zach made his call.

Staring at my cell, I frown before staring back at the woman pleadingly. "It only happened yesterday. Can't you search for her?"

She screws her face into a scowl and shakes her head. "I'm sorry, sir, it's hospital policy."

"Renny?"

Turning, Thea is standing behind me.

I close the gap between us and embrace her. "Are you okay?"

"How did you know?"

"Zach called me."

Thea pulls back but doesn't let go. "My phone died. I tried to call you." She looks over her shoulder, and standing about six feet from us is a member of the Savage Angels. "Then two members from your club showed up. Thank you, Renny."

I let go of Thea and approach the burly man. He stands over six feet tall, with bulging muscles and a bushy handlebar mustache framing his mouth like ape hanger handlebars.

He holds out his hand, and I shake it. "Nice to meet you, Renny. I'm Dozer. The president of our chapter sent me on behalf of the mother chapter."

"Thanks, man, I appreciate you taking care of what's mine."

He nods. "You're the closest anyone's come to getting near them. Whoever tried to take her out hasn't shown up here or at her apartment."

"You've got people on her home?"

"Yeah, in the shadows, just to be safe."

"Do we know who did it?"

Dozer peers around me to Thea. "She says she doesn't know, but..."

"You think she's lying?"

"I think she knows more than she's letting on." Dozer rocks back on his heels. "She's tough though, fought him off. Saved her friend from being gutted." He tilts his head to the side. "Well, completely gutted."

"Jesus," I mutter.

The big man shrugs and gives Thea a chin lift. "Yeah, it was gruesome, according to the kid."

"The kid? Zach?"

"Yeah, Repo is watching him in the waiting room three floors up."

"Thanks, man… appreciate it."

"It's cool, but our president will want to see you. You need to check-in. My orders are to stay close, which, if it's okay with you, I will."

"Thanks for asking, but seeing as I'm only a prospect, I'm sure I don't get a say."

He chuckles. "We look after our own."

"Renny?" calls Thea.

I extend a fist to Dozer, who bumps it with his, then I go back to Thea.

"He said you sent him?"

"Not me, Dane. Being in the MC has its perks."

"I've felt safer with them here. At one point, they manhandled a doctor who came out to talk to us." She smiles. "It was kind of funny."

"Can you take me to Zach?"

Her face falls a little. "Of course."

The three of us go up in the elevator. Thea keeps glancing at me, but she remains quiet. As soon as the doors open, Zach spots me and runs toward me. His arms wrap around my waist, and I rock back on one foot to stay upright. Zach squeezes tightly, his head buried in my stomach. "You came."

"I will always come for you." I stare at Thea. "And your mom. We're family."

Zach smiles. "And you sent Dozer and Repo to watch over us."

I tilt my head from side to side. "Well, sort of... the main thing is you're safe."

"Can we go back to Tourmaline now? Can we go home?"

Gritting my teeth together, I say, "That's up to

your mom." His face falls in disappointment. "Whatever your mom wants, she gets." I nod at Thea, who gives me a small smile.

I want them to come home with me, but I know if I tell Thea to pack her shit and leave town, she'll fight me every step of the way. This has to be her decision.

Thea holds out her hand to Zach, who lets me go and puts his hand in hers. Together, we walk over to the chairs in the waiting room. The chairs are covered in a dark blue material, a little scuffed, and the color probably hides a multitude of mishaps.

Hospitals make me uneasy. Though meant to heal, they harbor more dangerous germs than exist outside their walls. I always feel better when I can minimize my time spent inside one.

Repo leans against a wall and gives me a chin lift. Dozer stands near him, and they exchange pleasantries.

Pulling my wallet out of my pocket, I give Zach a ten-dollar bill. "Bud, why don't you and Repo find a vending machine? I could use something sugary like a Coke."

"Is this so you and Mom can talk?"

Smart kid.

"Yeah."

"Okay." He casts his mother a look, then walks over to the bikers.

From where I am, I can't hear what they are

saying, but Repo gives me a chin lift, and they walk down the hall.

"Tell me what happened."

Thea collapses in the chair. Great sobs come, and I put an arm around her, holding her close.

"It's okay," I whisper.

"It's not. None of it is. It was Samuel. He came out of the alley, and I froze. He had this expression on his face like the devil himself was controlling him. Mia put herself in front of me and pushed me hard to the ground. Samuel embedded his knife in her stomach and ripped upward." Thea shivers and clutches my shirt as she stares into my eyes. "He stabbed her so many times… I've never seen so much blood." Her mouth opens and closes, but nothing comes out.

"It's okay, honey, it's okay."

Shaking her head, she says, "I took too long to help her. Mia was screaming, and I was flat on my ass on the pavement, trying to figure out what to do. It's my fault. If I hadn't come back here, none of this would have happened."

Standing, I pull Thea to her feet while she cries. Eventually, she stops, and I rock her back and forth, patting her hair, trying to comfort her.

"Dozer said you fought him."

A hollow sound comes out of her. "Too little too late. Mia is my friend, and because of me, she might die."

"It's *because* of *you* she's still alive."

Looking into her eyes, I can tell she doesn't believe me, but she says nothing. Dozer whistles and flicks his head to the side, indicating Zach is returning.

Turning Thea around so her back is to him when he comes around the corner, I say, "Zach is coming. Pull it together for him."

Thea nods and walks behind me, brushing away her tears. Moving forward, I stop Zach before he gets near his mother. He holds up a Coke.

"Thanks, bud. It was a long drive... I need this." Smiling, I ask, "What did you get?"

"Sprite and a couple of candy bars."

"Anything in particular?" I ask, trying to buy his mother some time.

"A Mars bar for me and Snickers for Mom... she likes peanuts." He pulls a face.

"She's weird like that," I joke.

Thea appears beside me, her face a little red as she smiles down at Zach. "Thanks so much, honey, I'm starving." Her fake smile grows bigger. "And there's nothing wrong with peanuts."

Thea wraps an arm around Zach, and they sit together. Like the good kid he is, he opens his drink and offers it to her first.

Watching them, a burn begins to grow in my chest. I came so close to losing her. Taking a deep breath, I walk over to the two men. "I need to leave for a while."

Dozer puts a hand to my chest. "She told you who?"

"Yeah, an old friend."

Repo clicks his tongue. "You've gotta check in. Orders."

"I will. Tell me where to go, and I'm there."

Repo smiles. "I'll take you."

"It's cool, I can go on my own."

He belts out a laugh. "Not happening, *prospect*. You do as you're told, or you're out."

My jaw clenches, and I want to tell him to fuck off, but if I do, I'll be the shortest-serving Savage Angels MC member in history.

"Fine." I walk back to Thea and Zach, crouching in front of them. "I have to go. Dozer is going to stay with you. Go nowhere without him."

"Do you have to go, Dad?"

"Yeah, buddy." My eyes flick to Thea. "Be safe. I *will* be back." I kiss both on their foreheads.

"Don't do anything you'll regret." Thea reaches up and touches my face.

Cupping her face, I kiss her lips. "I won't."

I walk back to Repo, who escorts me to the elevators.

"She told you who did it, didn't she?"

"Yep."

"You going to share?"

I shake my head. "It's my problem to fix."

Repo raises his eyebrows and clears his throat. "You've got a lot to learn about the brotherhood. Lester is going to love you."

"Lester?"

"Our president."

"How the fuck is his name Lester? And come to think of it, why is Dane called Dane? Don't you guys all give each other handles? Like you, you're called Repo."

"Some do, some don't. If it makes you feel better, we call him Les for short. Dane, though, no one would be game enough to give him a nickname. The man's a powerhouse."

When we get to the parking lot, I point at Destiny's truck. "That's me."

"Nice."

"It's my sister's."

"Is she single?"

"No, she's engaged to Kade."

"Cantrill?"

"Yeah."

"He's a good guy."

We walk to the truck. "How do you know him?"

"Kade, JJ, and Zeke used to visit on the regular. Shame about JJ."

Opening the truck, we both get inside. "I don't know him."

"And you won't. He was killed a while back. Rumor has it he's the reason they finally picked a chapter to settle down with, after he died, Kade and Zeke needed a place to call home. JJ is buried in Tourmaline, maybe they stayed to be close to him."

Repo gives the occasional grunt and points in the direction he wants me to go. Soon the scenery descends into dilapidated warehouses and rusty chain-link fences. One fence stands out with the Savage Angels' logo displayed boldly across it and has razor wire curled menacingly along the top, ready to shred intruders. The concrete clubhouse beyond looks cold and sterile, devoid of anything remotely welcoming. It's a bunker designed for function, not comfort—nothing like the warm, woody exterior of the Tourmaline clubhouse. The message is clear—this is not a place to get comfortable. It's a fortress for battle-hardened bikers.

"Homey," I say.

"It is what it is. We've been here for nearly a year. It's nicer on the inside. With the Tourmaline Chapter's help, we were able to buy this place outright. It's big enough to service vehicles, and we can make as much noise as we want, seeing as it's in an industrial area. You probably noticed how rundown it is on the way in. This means we can buy the surrounding buildings and lots cheap."

"And having an MC who is loud probably doesn't help with prices either?"

Repo grins. "You ain't as dumb as you look."

There's only one parking space left, and it's next to a long line of bikes. The truck has barely stopped when Repo climbs out and walks inside. When I'm out of the truck, a couple of the brothers greet me with a two-finger salute and chin lifts.

Walking inside, on the left is an office, and on the right are two bays for working on cars. The receptionist, a woman in her forties with too much makeup and a black tank top with the Savage Angels' logo on the front, is on the telephone. She points to a door behind her without making eye contact with me.

I open the door and enter what appears to be a bar space. Tables, chairs, and two pool tables fill the large room, yet only two people are inside—Repo leaning on the bar and another man I don't recognize. The walls are painted black and decorated with Savage Angels' posters and flags. The concrete floor is polished to a shine with a drain in the center. Repo said it was better on the inside, but to me, this cavernous room feels sterile, like a slaughterhouse where you could be gutted and your remains hosed down the drain with no one knowing.

"Prez, this is Renny."

The man turns. His salt-and-pepper beard is neatly trimmed, and his long hair is pulled back in a ponytail, showing off the crow and reaper tattoos covering his neck and arms. The black leather cut displays his presidency patch and various embroidered logos indicating his years in the club. Though relaxed, leaning against the bar, his piercing blue eyes scan the room, missing nothing. He has an air of quiet authority. His face is weathered, hinting at a hard life, but he carries himself with a calm, steady confidence.

He holds out his hand. "Nice to meet you, Renny. I'm Les." His voice is gravelly but commanding.

"Thanks for looking out for my family."

"Repo tells me you're on a revenge mission."

He's nothing if not straight to the point.

"It's my mess. I want to be the one to clean it up."

Les walks slowly around the bar and pulls down a bottle of whiskey. "You drink?"

"No, thanks."

He pours himself a glass, then takes a sip. "Dane called in a favor to babysit your family. The man doesn't put himself out for just anyone." He points to my cut. "You're only a prospect. Why would he do that?"

It's one of those situations where I want to tell him to fuck off, but I'm part of this now, and knowing Dane stuck out his neck for me means I need to handle this diplomatically. After weighing my words in my mind, I decide honesty is best way.

"My old crew framed me for murder. I only recently got out on a technicality."

"Where'd you do your time?" Repo asks.

"Eight years in Glenford."

Les' head jerks back in surprise, and Repo lets out a long whistle.

"Not an easy place to survive." Les throws back the rest of his drink. "I did a year. Got shanked twice, spent most of my time in the hospital ward."

"It pays to have friends." I slip my hands into my jeans pockets. "Have you heard of Sergio Alvarez?"

Les splays both hands on the bar top and leans forward. "Leader of the Juarez Cartel. We were in business with them."

"Not anymore?"

"No, drugs are an easy way to make money, but they can poison an MC. Our previous president couldn't see we were imploding. Too many of us got addicted, and it became easy for law enforcement to have brothers turn on their colors, and too many of us ended up in prison."

He doesn't say it, but judging by his demeanor and the fact he said he did a year, he was one of the men who went in because of a traitor.

"How do you afford all this?"

"Not dealing. We own several of the garages in and around town as well as strip clubs and tattoo parlors. Where once only the underside of society got inked, now everyone has one. They've become socially acceptable, and the young ones pay a fortune for them." He studies me, then says, "Dane helped us get out of that life. Sure, occasionally we run guns, and maybe some of those runs have the odd kilo or two, but as a rule, we're clean."

"Alvarez is big time. We don't need the heat," agrees Repo.

Holding up a hand, I say, "Let me explain. Do you remember years ago when the Juarez Cartel cleaned house, and a sum of money went missing?"

Les shakes his head, and Repo shrugs.

"It was me and my crew. We stole three million off him."

Les belts out a laugh. "And that's why your crew turned on you?"

"Yeah, they wanted the money for themselves, but I'd hidden it."

"I'm confused. If you stole the money, why aren't you dead?" Repo asks.

"Sergio doesn't know it was me. I pointed him in the right direction after I got out of prison. He and I are friends... well, sort of. I saved his life in prison. He has no reason *not* to believe me. And I planted the money in one of my old associate's homes."

"You're letting Alvarez do your dirty work for you?" Les asks.

"I'm trying to stay clean, but either he doesn't believe me or—"

"He's figured out it was you?" finishes Repo.

"Maybe. But it was one of my old crew who went after my woman and son."

Repo turns and stares at Les, and something

unspoken passes between them. Eventually, Les nods and looks at me.

"What are you planning to do?"

"I'm going to reach out to Sergio and find out if I'm blown. If I'm not, I'm going to ask if I can help in wiping them off the face of the planet."

"Won't that make it obvious you were part of it?" Repo asks without turning around.

"Or I'll appear as though I'm loyal to Sergio."

Les taps the side of his temple. "You're playing a dangerous game. You don't want to be tied to the Juarez Cartel. They'll chew you up and spit you out."

"If it means my family is safe, I'm willing to do it."

Lester crosses his arms over his chest. "Yeah, but you're with us now, and we don't want the heat. No one wants to be in bed with the Juarez Cartel. If you open that bottle, we might not be able to close it. You need to find another way, brother."

Anger rises within me. I'm not in prison anymore. *No one* owns me or tells me what to do.

Les moves around the bar, hands raised as if sensing my imminent burst of anger. "All we're saying is it's not just about you anymore. You're part of something bigger. Let us help."

For so long, I've relied on myself. I joined the Savage Angels for the safety in numbers, but perhaps Les is right. Dane called in a favor to protect my family, so the least I can do is try to work with the MC.

"What did you have in mind?"

Les raises his eyebrows. "First, we need to know who it was who went after your family."

"Samuel Perth."

Les faces Repo. "Go do your thing."

When our meeting was over, members of the MC came into the room. Repo has been gone for the better part of two hours. I've gone from patiently waiting to pacing back and forth like a caged animal.

"For fuck's sake, man, have a drink, play pool or darts, or grab a club angel but stop your pacing. It's starting to grate on my nerves."

Glancing up, there's a large black man with a shaved head and emerald green eyes. He's a patched-in member and clearly pissed off with me. No one else pays him any attention, so maybe this is his normal frame of mind.

"It's been two hours."

He shrugs, his lips turning down. "It'll take as long as it takes."

"Easy for you to say. It's not your family on the line."

He stands, muscles straining against his white T-shirt and extends a hand to me. "Razor."

"I'm Renny."

We shake, and he sits. "Take a seat."

Feeling as though I have too much energy to sit in one place, I shake my head.

"I wasn't asking, prospect."

Frustrated, I do as he asks but glare at him.

Razor laughs. "You keep looking at me like that, and I'll think you've got a crush on me."

"I'm about to lose my mind."

Razor leans forward, his T-shirt straining against the motion. "Your family is safe. Dozer is bringing them here." His eyes stare over my head. "In fact, here they are now."

Swiveling in my chair, Thea and Zach walk through the doors. Standing, I walk quickly to them and crush them in a hug.

"How's Mia?"

Thea's hand finds mine. "She's stable. The doctor says it's up to her now."

Threading my fingers with hers, I lift it to my lips and kiss her knuckles. "Good."

Tears well in her eyes, she shakes her head and glances down at Zach who's latched onto my leg.

"We were thinking we'd like to come home."

The burn in my chest, which has slowly turned into an inferno, instantly disappears.

"Home to Tourmaline?" I ask tentatively.

Zach nods, and Thea says, "If you'll have us."

Letting go of her hand, I put my arm around her and say into her hair, "All day, every day."

Razor clears his throat loudly to get my attention. The man is standing. He dips his chin to his chest and looks at Thea with raised eyebrows.

Releasing Thea, I say, "Razor, this is Thea, and this..." I point toward Zach, "... is my son, Zach."

Zach lets me go and shakes hands with the huge man. "Nice to meet you, sir."

Razor laughs. "Call me Razor, little man."

Thea holds out her hand to him, and he hesitates for a moment before he shakes it. His eyes come to me when he releases her.

"You and the woman need to come with me. Les wants to see you."

"What about Zachary?" asks Thea.

"Dozer is going to get him something to eat and play pool with him."

Thea stares at me. "Is he safe?"

Razor answers for me, "He's safer here than anywhere else. The room is filled with your new family. We take care of our own."

She glances between us and then looks down at our son. "Are you okay here by yourself?"

"I'm not alone, Mom. I'll be with Dozer."

Thea raises her eyebrows in surprise. "Okay."

Razor walks across the brightly lit bar, his footsteps heightened on the polished concrete. He approaches the back wall, where a door has been cunningly disguised to blend seamlessly into the dark wood paneling. Only Razor's familiarity betrays its presence. Beyond lies a spacious room lit by a single stark bulb. A large round table surrounded by a mismatched assortment of chairs occupies the center. The table sits atop an elaborate rug, its once vibrant colors faded and patterns obscured by years of use. Three more unmarked doors lead off into unknown rooms.

"Sit. Les won't be long."

"Thanks, Razor."

He cocks his head to the side and gives me the once-over. "You're welcome, prospect." Turning, he leaves the room, so it's only Thea and me.

Thea sits, and I move a chair closer to her so I can hold her hands.

"Are you okay?"

"Yes."

"Did Samuel say anything?"

She shakes her head, eyes on my chest. "No."

Her one-word answers betray the turmoil she must be feeling.

Cupping her face, I tilt her head so she's looking into my eyes. "I'm sorry I didn't tell you about the Savage Angels. I should have. But with our past history, I wanted you to get to know them before I told you. It was a mistake on my part, one I wish I could undo."

A tear runs down her face. "Oh, Renny, I'm sorry too. I shouldn't have run. The way Dozer and Repo came to protect us showed me that maybe I don't know what an MC is all about. I wouldn't have blamed you if you'd abandoned us."

"Never."

Thea puts her hand over mine. "I think we need a do-over. One where we are honest with each other, and even if we think the other won't like it, we need to speak our truths."

"Agreed."

Leaning in, I press my lips to hers. A door opens, disturbing our solitude. Les walks in with Repo behind him.

"Ahh, good you're here," Les says, staring at Thea. He sits near us, and Repo sits opposite him. "Repo made some calls."

"Discreetly," chimes in Repo.

"No one knows you were behind the theft. Turns out Sergio went after your old associates. Two got away, Samuel Perth and Hunter Johns."

"*Great,*" says Thea. "The sociopaths live."

"You two are clean." Les leans back, eyes on Thea. "You were a part of it too, weren't you?"

"Yes."

He smiles and locks eyes with Repo, who nods.

"Told you it was a seven-man crew."

Staring at Repo, I ask, "How did you know?"

"Logistics, but not everyone's mind works like

mine. No one else will figure it out, especially when there's chatter about the five of them."

"Chatter?"

Repo taps the bar top. "The prison network is like gossip for little old ladies. You plant a seed and let it run. Soon, everyone knows who did it, how they did it, and why they didn't spend the money. All it takes is a few lifers saying they heard from so and so, and soon it's fact."

"So we're clean?"

"Yeah. It was smart of you to plant the money in one of their houses."

Les taps the table. "It won't be long until the Juarez Cartel has the other two in their clutches. You're safe to go home."

Standing, I hold out my hand to Les. "I guess this means I owe you?"

Les shakes his head. "Nope. Dane did right by you... you do right by Dane."

"Can we go?" Thea asks.

"Yes. Wherever Perth and Johns are, they aren't in our city. The cartel may have already ended them. All we need to do is wait for the bodies to drop. The other three have made the news. Tortured." Les pauses and stares at Thea. "I won't go into too much detail, but eventually a tire was placed around them, and they were set on fire." His mouth turns down. "Not a pretty way to go."

Thea shivers. "No."

I pull her up, and we walk through the clubhouse to Zach. He's laughing with Razor and has a plate of fries in front of him.

"Mom, want some fries?"

Thea ruffles his hair and takes one off his plate. "Time to go."

Zach stands and smiles at Razor. "Thanks for the food."

"You're welcome, little man." Razor's eyes flick to me. "Don't be a stranger, prospect."

Together, we walk outside.

"I'm beat. How about we get a motel? We can decide tomorrow what we are going to do."

Thea nods. "I could sleep. Zachary, honey, what about you?"

"Can we get ice cream?"

Thea looks at me. "Somewhere with room service?"

"I'm hungry too," I reply with an affirmative head shake.

"Aunty Destiny let you use her truck?"

"Yeah, she missed you too and wants you home."

Zach smiles, and as a family, we pile into the vehicle.

CHAPTER 26

RENNY

A month later, we're all settled into our new apartment in Tourmaline. I'm at the Savage Angels' garage under a car when my phone rings. Sliding out, I pull my phone from my pocket and see it's an unknown number. I hit the button to answer the call.

"Hello."

"Renny, how goes it?"

Sergio Alvarez's voice filters down the line.

"Sergio?"

"Yes."

Sitting up, I check my surroundings. The man makes me nervous. "I'm good. What can I do for you, and how did you get my number?"

He chuckles. "I keep tabs on my friends," he pauses, then says, "I got my money back. After your call about one of them, it was easy to see who his crew was. They did a number of jobs together. Unfortunately, we only got three of them, but they won't be around to brag about it to anyone anymore."

"Are you happy?" It makes me uneasy that he only got three, which means two have slipped past him, or he knows I'm involved and is playing with me.

"No. Two are missing, but we'll find them. I wanted to thank you. Over the years, there's been a lot of theories about who stole it and why. It's nice to know I can count on my friends."

Rubbing my face, I say, "We were friends. I'm not sure what we are, but life is good for me, Sergio. I have a woman and a son, and I'm working hard and keeping my nose clean. Prison is not somewhere I ever want to go back to."

Sergio laughs. "And yet you survived in there better than most. Can I count on you if I ever need a friend?"

Sergio Alvarez is not a man you want to say no to, so I reply with, "You are and always will be a man of power, but I'm not a player in the outside world. I've no connections or power plays here. Sure, if you want a friend to shoot the shit, I'm here, but anything else? No, I can't help you."

"That's what I love about you, Renny. You were always straight with me. Good luck, amigo, and if you ever need anything, you know how to find me."

Sergio ends the call, and I let out a sigh.

"Dude, you okay?" asks Judge.

"Yeah, just an old friend saying goodbye."

An uneasy feeling snakes its way up my spine. Sergio said he only got three of them, which means there are two left. Will they realize it was me who dimed them out? If they are caught alive, will they talk about me and Thea, or will they die quickly?

Judge nudges me with his boot. "Time for lunch. You don't look good."

"Fuck you, man."

Judge chuckles. "Nah, I've got a woman, but thanks."

Judge walks away, and I have this urge to make sure Thea and Zach are okay. Standing, I walk into the office where Addy is looking over paperwork.

"Hey, Addy, I'm taking an early lunch. I should have the car I'm working on fixed by the end of the day."

She looks up at me. "Okay, I'll let the others know." Then she goes back to her paperwork.

My hands are covered in grease, but I don't bother to wash up. Instead, I hurry toward Betty's Café. Looking in the window, Thea is laughing with Howie. She spots me and comes to the door.

"Hey, handsome, you here for lunch?"

Relief washes over me, and I nod. "Yep. Can you take a break too?"

Thea looks over her shoulder then back at me. “It’s not busy, so probably, but I’ll need to check with the boss.”

Howie yells, “Thea, take a break!”

Laughing, I enter the café.

“What do you want?” Thea asks.

“Hamburger.”

“Go on out back, and I’ll bring it to you.”

Moving through the café, I sit at Howie’s picnic table and send up a silent prayer to the gods, thanking them for keeping my family safe.

CHAPTER 27

Thea

The days, weeks, and months after the attack on Mia all blur together into one long, hazy period of time. As soon as she was well enough to travel, Renny packed up her and Tyrone's belongings and moved them to Tourmaline.

Gus, the kind gentleman who rented me my apartment, had another unit become available and generously allowed Tyrone and Mia to rent it. Since she can work remotely from anywhere, and Tyrone postponed his studies, they had no reason to remain where they were. The change of scenery to Tourmaline feels like a refreshing new start after the trauma of the attack for all of us.

I step out of the steamy shower, the hot water having washed away the grime from another long shift at the diner. Wrapping myself in a soft towel, I catch my reflection in the fogged mirror and realize I'm smiling. Tonight, I get to experience life again. Zachary and Renny are chatting in the living room as I get ready, their laughter filtering through the thin walls of our little apartment. We're all going to the Savage Angels' clubhouse for a party. My heart feels full for the first time in years. Dirt offered to pick Tyrone and Mia up, the gruff biker having taken a liking to her.

As I pull on my favorite dress and touch up my makeup, I marvel at how everything has fallen into place—this job, this home, and these friends who feel like family. For so long, I focused on surviving and getting through each day. But now, with Renny and Zachary living under the same roof, I remember what it feels like to truly live. Tonight will be a celebration of our new lives.

Walking into our living room, Zachary lets out a wolf whistle, and Renny stands, giving me the once-over.

"Do I look okay?"

Renny stalks around me, a predatory smile on his face. "No. You're stunning."

Heat infuses my cheeks as I smooth my red floral dress, and I ask, "I'm not too overdone?"

Renny shakes his head. "Nope."

"Dad's right, Mom, you look good."

Smiling at the two men in my life, I nod. "Well, okay then, shall we go?"

"I thought we'd walk. Is that okay?"

"Makes sense, then we can both have a drink." I bend to pick up my purse and then link my arm with Renny. "You look good too."

Renny chuckles. "We all scrub up nicely."

The night air is warm, and we walk to the other end of town, where the MC clubhouse is located, as a family.

A police cruiser pulls up alongside us.

Bending to see who's inside, I wave at the sheriff. "Hey, Carlos. Are you coming to the party?"

"No, I'm on my way home to Izzy. Tell Dane to make sure the party stays in the compound."

Renny moves me away from the cruiser. "We don't run errands for the local PD."

Carlos frowns. "Fine, I'll just drive down there and tell him myself."

"Wait." Renny stares up at the night sky in annoyance. "I'll tell him."

Carlos grins. "Much appreciated! And try to keep the noise to a minimum."

Renny gives him a thumbs-up, and Carlos gives me a wave and continues on his way.

"He's a nice man. Good tipper."

"He's the local sheriff, and I don't have much time for the law."

"Is he a bad man?" asks Zachary.

"No, honey. Like all walks of life, there are good and bad, but Sheriff Morales is one of the good guys."

"And you're sure of that?" challenges Renny.

With a laugh, I say, "Yes." I put an arm around Zachary. "Remember to always make up your own mind about people. Take your dad, for example. With all his tattoos and his happy disposition, people think he's bad, but we *know* he's not."

The pulse of bass throbs in the air as we approach the Savage Angels' clubhouse. With each step along Main Street, the music grows louder, the rhythmic thump calling us toward the party within. I can make out the fuzzy blend of rock music over the distinctive rumble of motorcycles. Men's raucous laughter drifts on the night breeze, mingling with the clinking of bottles and glasses. The amber glow of fire barrels bathes the exterior chain-link fence in flickering light. Renny puts his arm around me as we walk through the gates.

"Hey, Renny!"

Turning around, Tobias is jogging toward us, his hand raised in greeting. We stop while he catches up with us.

Renny holds out his hand, and Tobias shakes it. "Hey, Tobias, what brings you here?"

"I'm sort of an honorary member."

"Really?" asks Renny.

Tobias chuckles. "No." He gestures over his shoulder to a group of scantily-clad women who are getting out of a bus. "Some of my girls wanted to come, so I'm here to make sure they're okay."

Tobias puts his hands in his pockets, waiting for the women to catch up. He's tall like Renny, well-built but a little too pretty, with his long hair pulled back into a bun at the base of his neck. He also wears silver rings on each finger. I suppose he looks like the sort of man who would run a strip club.

A loud noise pierces the air, and Tobias goes up on the balls of his feet and then flies through the air backward. Renny yells, pushes me to the ground, then grabs Zachary and runs behind a car. I hit the ground hard, falling near Tobias. Blood spurts out of a hole where his left eye was. Screams pierce the air, and chaos takes over as the men of the MC run toward the danger. Bullets sound like firecrackers, so many of them firing in quick succession.

Renny appears beside me. "Move!" he bellows.

"Tobias!" I scream as I stare at the man's once-pretty face.

"No time!" Renny pulls me toward a car where Zachary is hiding. "Stay down!"

He runs back toward the danger, and I stare at Zachary, clutching my hand. "Honey, give me your T-shirt." He slips it over his head. "Whatever happens, you stay here. You stay down."

Keeping low to the ground, I make my way back to Tobias. Wadding up the T-shirt, I place it over his face. A groan escapes him.

"It's okay, you're okay."

There are at least a dozen men in front of me, guns drawn. Shouts and screams pierce the air, and Kat appears beside me.

"How bad?" she asks as she kneels in the dirt.

"You shouldn't be here." My eyes go to her round belly.

"Neither should you."

Dane appears beside her, a gun in his hands. "Darlin', we've gotta move."

"Tobias, he's hurt."

Dane looks down, hands the gun to Kat, and scoops Tobias up as though he weighs nothing.

"Time to move," barks out Dane.

"Zachary," I yell as I keep my hands on Tobias. "Come here. *Now!*"

Zachary appears beside us as we hurry toward Dane's truck. Kat pulls open the heavy tailgate, and Dane gently lays Tobias down on the cold metal truck bed.

"Can you stay with him?" Dane asks, his brow furrowed with concern.

"If you keep my son safe with you in the front," I reply.

Dane nods, grabbing Zachary's small hand in one of his large, calloused ones, and wraps his other arm around his wife's waist. "Get in the truck," he urges gruffly. He glances over his shoulder at me, his icy-blue eyes piercing. "We're taking Tobias to Doc Jordan."

Carefully, I position Tobias' head in my lap, brushing his blood-soaked hair back from his forehead. Judge climbs into the truck bed with us, a shotgun clenched in his fist. I press my back up against the rear window of the cab, holding the injured man steady.

Judge glances down at Tobias, his lips curling back in a vicious snarl. "Drive!"

The truck lurches forward violently as we speed out of the Savage Angels' compound, loose gravel pinging against the undercarriage. I search the chaotic crowd as they reluctantly part to let us through, but I don't see Renny among the sea of cuts and beards. There are two bodies lying motionless on the ground near the clubhouse entrance. And in the distance, there are pulsing red and blue lights of the local police heading down Main Street.

Dane takes an immediate right, then a left as he speeds through town. When we pull up in front of an older two-story home, an elderly man rushes out with a black bag. He climbs into the back of the truck and locks eyes with me.

"I need to examine him."

Nodding, I let go of Zachary's once-white T-shirt, now soaked a deep crimson. The doctor lifts it and swears to himself.

Dane appears next to the truck bed. "How bad?"

"Gunshot wound to the head. No telling how bad

it is right now." The older doctor stares at Dane. "We need to get to the hospital. I can't do much for him here." He opens his bag and pulls out some gauze, putting it over the bullet wound. "He needs to go to the Baptist Hospital in Pearl."

"Is it safe to move him in this?"

The doctor shakes his head. "We need to keep him as still as possible. The bullet is still in there. There's no exit wound."

A scream sounds from the front of the truck. Dane runs around the vehicle, and I peer through the back window. Kat is hunched over, clutching her stomach, and Zachary's face appears in front of me.

"Mom! I think she's having the baby."

"No. It's too early," states Dane as he wrenches open the door.

Doc Jordan stares me in the eyes. "Keep the pressure on… I'll just be a minute."

The older man climbs out of the truck bed, and Judge's cell phone rings.

He answers it, "Speak." He glances at me. "We're at Doc Jordan's." He's standing and moves further toward the edge of the truck bed. "We need to get to the Baptist Hospital."

Judge drops his phone and raises the shotgun to his shoulder. Staring into the darkness, I can see at least three figures running toward us.

Fear crawls up my throat, and I search for

Zachary in the back of the truck. “Get down!”

Zachary’s little face disappears, and he stares once more at the impending threat closing the distance.

“Judge! It’s Dirt.”

Judge swears and lowers the shotgun. “I nearly shot you, you stupid son of a bitch.”

Dirt comes into the light of the dimly lit street. “Well, that’s one way to move up the ranks.” He keeps going to Dane, who has both hands on the top of his head, staring at his wife. “Prez, speak to me.”

“Tobias is injured, and Doc says we need to get him to the hospital.”

“Kat’s gone into labor.” Doc Jordan moves out of the door of the vehicle.

“She still has two months.”

Doc reaches out and puts a hand on Dane’s bulging bicep. “Yeah, but the babies don’t know that.” He glances at Tobias and then back to Dane. “Get in the back. Judge, you’re driving, but I need you to keep it steady. Try as hard as you can to avoid the bumps in the road. I’m going to ride in the back with Tobias. Dane, you keep your wife calm.”

“I can hear you,” states Kat.

The doctor grins. “Good, then keep calm. We’re all going on a drive.”

“What about Renny?”

Dirt looks at me. “He’s fine. Sheriff Morales won’t let him leave. Apparently, the gunmen were people he knew."

"But he's not hurt?"

Dirt shakes his head. "No, he's fine. I could take you to him?"

Doc Jordan climbs back into the bed of the truck. "I'm sorry, little lady, but I'm going to need you for the drive to the hospital. We're going to have to keep him steady."

"I can do that."

Dirt climbs into the truck. "I could take over for her."

"You can't, but no matter, I'm going to need both of you."

"Renny doesn't know where we are."

The other two men are on their phones, and one of them nods at Dirt.

"They'll let him know."

"Judge, move out," orders Doc Jordan.

The truck roars down the empty road as I cradle Tobias' limp body in my arms. His breathing is shallow, each ragged inhale a struggle. The makeshift bandage on his head is soaked through with blood, and I can feel it pooling beneath us. I apply pressure, willing him to hold on for a little longer. We're almost to the Baptist Hospital.

Kat sits rigid in the passenger seat, one hand on her swollen belly and the other gripping the door handle until her knuckles turn white. She winces every now and again, gritting her teeth at the pain. In the rearview mirror, her eyes meet mine. They glisten with unshed tears, but her jaw is set with determination.

Judge pushes the gas pedal to the floor, the truck's engine groaning in protest. His eyes stay locked on the road ahead. Beside me, Dirt scans the darkness over the barrel of his shotgun, ready to defend our flight to save Tobias' life.

Up ahead, the hospital sign glows like a beacon in the night. "We're almost there… just hang on," I whisper to Tobias' motionless form.

His life now hangs by the thinnest of threads, but we will not let it sever. Not tonight. The Baptist Hospital rises to meet us as we race toward whatever future awaits beyond those doors. We park in Emergency, and people rush out of the double doors. Some go to the front of the truck, and others take Tobias off me. Doc Jordan is barking orders about his patients, and they are hurried inside, leaving Zachary, Dirt, and me outside.

Tobias' blood drenches my dress, staining it a dark, ominous crimson. As I struggle to rise, Dirt extends a welcoming hand, his gritty palm pulling me to my feet. Zachary emerges from the truck and swiftly makes his way to the rear. Dirt leaps from the truck bed, landing gracefully on the ground before offering me a steadying hand. With his help, I climb down, and then we walk into the hospital.

The emergency room is in a state of chaos. Kat is rushed to an elevator with Dane following close behind. Tobias is on a gurney, one of his hands dangling off the side, his large frame barely contained on the bed.

Doc Jordan is standing off to one side, the older man looking concerned as he listens to a younger doctor bark orders.

A tall woman in scrubs walks into the small area. "What do we have?"

"Gunshot wound to the head."

She smiles. "Sounds like it's one for me and the O.R."

Doc Jordan steps forward. "His name is Tobias Dupont."

"Are you a relative?" she asks.

"No, I'm his doctor. He got shot in Tourmaline. I helped deliver him to you. You're the new hotshot out of Chicago. Dr. Grills, he's got a lot of friends," Doc Jordan gestures over his shoulder to Dirt who scowls at her. "You'd best fix him, or you'll be going home to Chicago and maybe in the baggage compartment."

The doctor's mouth drops open, and then she

focuses back on Tobias. “Okay, people, let’s move him!”

Doc Jordan joins us. “Come on, let’s get you cleaned up.” He takes me by the arm.

“What was all that about, Doc?” asks Dirt.

“She’s young, very good, and a little too cocky. The fear of God won’t hurt her.”

“Except it wasn’t the fear of God but the fear of the Savage Angels.”

“Close enough.”

CHAPTER 28

RENNY

Sheriff Morales kept me and the rest of the Savage Angels at the clubhouse for hours. Samuel and Hunter lie dead in the dirt outside the gates. Eventually, everyone who had a gun was arrested and taken to the sheriff's station, and because of my connection to the two men, I was placed in a room alone. At first, I yelled and demanded to be released so I could check on my family. Then Rush arrived with Destiny, and they threatened to sue the sheriff and his entire office, but he laughed and invited them to sit with me.

Together we sit, in silence, waiting to be released.

The door opens, the sheriff walks in, and sits opposite me. "Tell me again how you knew the two men."

"Samuel and Hunter were childhood friends."

"Sheriff, is my client under arrest?" asks Destiny.

He looks at her, shakes his head, and stares into my eyes. "Do old friends often try to kill you?"

"Sheriff, this line of questioning is quite frankly absurd," interjects Rush.

He ignores him and says, "Renny, answer the question."

"I don't know."

The sheriff leans back in his chair. "I've done some digging with some associates in Chicago, and apparently, they were tied to the Juarez Cartel. Do you know anything about that?"

"Not a thing."

"Really?" His eyebrows shoot up to his hairline. "You shared a cell with Sergio Alvarez."

"For a crime he didn't commit," Destiny replies.

The sheriff holds up his hand. "Do you know Sergio Alvarez?"

"Yes."

Rush holds up a hand. "Renny, do not answer any of his questions."

"You seem to be the common denominator."

Leaning forward, I say, "I haven't spoken to them in over eight years. As for Sergio, I haven't seen him since he left Glenford." Spreading my hands out, I smile at the man. "I can't help you, sheriff."

He stands. "You're free to go."

"That's it?"

Morales nods. "Your family is waiting outside."

Hurrying from the room and through the sheriff's station, my heart races as I catch sight of Thea and Zachary in the waiting area. Overcome with emotion, Thea's arms encircle my neck, and I cling to her tightly, a rush of love and relief flooding over me.

"How's Tobias?" I ask into her neck.

Thea leans back and pulls Zach into our circle. "Still in surgery when we left."

Placing a hand on Zach's head, I stare down at him. "Buddy, what are you wearing?"

"Doc Jordan got it for me at the hospital. Mom used my T-shirt on Tobias."

"How's Kat?" asks Destiny.

"Did Kat get hit?" I ask.

Thea shakes her head. "No, she went into labor." Thea looks around me to Destiny. "The babies and Kat are fine. Dane, on the other hand, looks ten years older. Anyone would think he gave birth."

"He loves her," states Destiny. "She had a hard time with the last pregnancy... he'll be worried, is all."

"Who's got his kids?" I ask.

"They were at home with Bear and Shaz. They're fine." Destiny nods toward the exit. "Come on, let's get you home."

Not needing to be asked twice, I move my family outside to the sidewalk.

"If they call you in again, I'm your first call. Got it?" Rush points at me. "Come on, Destiny, let's get you home."

He holds out his arm to her, and they walk down Main Street.

"Does the sheriff want to talk to you again?" Thea asks.

"I don't think so." With a tilt of my head, I move us toward home. "How you doing, buddy?"

Zach looks up at me, clearly tired. "I'm okay."

With an arm around Thea and one on Zach's shoulder, we walk the short distance to our apartment. As soon as we get through the door, he peels off the shirt Doc Jordan found for him and drops it in the trash.

"Mom, do I have to have a shower?"

"No, honey, you can have one in the morning."

He nods and staggers into his bedroom.

"Is he okay?"

Thea nods. "He didn't see much. Everything happened so fast." She looks down at her dress. "I loved this dress."

"We could wash it?"

Her lips turn down at the corners. "I don't think I could ever wear it again without thinking about this night."

"I'll buy you a new one."

Thea turns around, giving me her back. "Unzip me?"

The zipper comes down easily, and Thea lets the dress fall to the floor. Dried blood coats most of her midsection. I put my hands on her shoulders and guide her toward the bathroom. Reaching in, I turn on the shower, wait until the water is warm, then step out of the way.

"Hop in, babe. Let's get you cleaned up."

Thea unclasps her bra, pushes her panties down her legs, and climbs into the shower. The water at her feet turns a muddy red as the blood goes down the drain.

"Scrub my back?" She squirts bodywash onto a sponge and hands it to me.

Peeling off my shirt, I clean her back and down her legs. Thea turns, and I do her front as well.

"You're all wet."

"Doesn't matter."

"I'm so tired."

Stripping out of my boots and jeans, I hold her close as the warm water washes over us. We stay like that until the water goes cold.

After we dry off and are in bed, we snuggle together. I whisper to her in the darkness, "It was Samuel and Hunter. They came for me."

"For us."

"Maybe."

"They were after the money."

"I don't have it."

Thea places a hand on my chest. "I don't care. All

I ever wanted was you and Zachary, and I have you both. We'll get by."

"There's more... things I haven't told you. In prison, to survive, I owe three men favors. Two can wait as they're still serving time, but one is out, and I owe him a debt. Kade offered to put me in touch with a mafioso, Salvatore Agostino. He thinks he can help with Brandon, but it'll probably mean I'm going to owe Agostino."

"Owe him what?"

"No idea."

Thea sits up, resting her arms on my chest. "Whatever it is, we'll face it together."

"You sure about that?"

Thea lays back down and moves her head against my chest. "Yep."

"Give me a sec."

I move out of her embrace, stand, and pad over to the dresser. Opening a drawer, I pull out the worn velvet pouch and kneel beside the bed.

"This was meant for you a long time ago, but the universe had other ideas for us. I know now it was always going to be yours, and it doesn't matter what we've done or what we're going to do so long as we do it together."

I slip the ring out of the pouch and hold it up to her.

Thea gasps.

"Thea North, will you marry me?"

She sits bolt upright and takes the ring from me. "You had this the entire time?"

"Is that a yes or no?"

Tears glisten in her eyes as I hold my breath, waiting for her to answer me.

When it finally comes, her voice is soft and filled with love. "Yes."

Joy washes over me as I take the ring and slip it over her finger. Thea stares at it for a moment then scoots across the bed and kisses me.

"It's always been you, Renny. Our love has weathered many storms, but in the end, we found our way back to each other." A smile plays on her lips. "Now kiss me and make me yours."

"You always were."

"And now I always will be."

CHAPTER 29

DIRT

Forty-eight hours later, and I'm waiting outside ICU for news of Tobias. A bunch of women from The Cherry are waiting in the cafeteria. Some came straight from work, dressed scantily, but all of them are beautiful, and the one thing they have in common is their love for Tobias.

"Any change?" asks Destiny as she stands next to me.

"No."

"He's stable, though?"

I know she needs me to tell her he's going to be okay, but no one knows.

"He's a tough son of a bitch."

Destiny reaches out and places a hand on my arm. "*He is.*"

"I need some air. You'll stay here in case he

wakes up?"

Destiny nods. "Bring me back a coffee?"

"Sure will."

Striding for the elevators, I get inside and hit the button to take me to the maternity ward. The elevator dings, and I step out into a calm space. Compared to the ICU, it's homey with soft carpets and lighting.

Kat has her own room and standing outside guarding her is Kade. I walk to it, and he steps aside so I can enter. Inside, Dane is asleep in a chair, snoring softly, but Kat is awake with one of her babies in her arms.

"Hey," I whisper.

Kat smiles at me. "Hey, you." She looks down lovingly at the bundle in her arms. "Blaze meet Uncle Dirt." Kat moves the blanket away from his face.

"Aww, you did good, woman."

She gestures toward a crib, and I see another baby all wrapped up inside. "Uncle Dirt, that's Gunner. He's the oldest and like his little brother, he's doing so well."

"You make pretty babies."

Kat grins. "You say all the right things."

"When can you go home?"

"The doctors want to keep an eye on them for a few more days. Even though they were early, they're doing great."

"Has the press bothered you?"

Kat shakes her head. "Not with the boys guarding all the entrances. Dane made sure we have our privacy."

"Do you want me to take Blaze off you so you can sleep?"

Kat scrunches up her face. "I know I should say yes, but I like holding onto them. They get so big so fast, and boys don't want their momma cuddling them when they get older. I miss it so much."

Bending, I place a kiss on her temple. "You do you."

"Are you kissing my woman?"

Turning, Dane is sitting up, rubbing his eyes.

"Just saying congratulations."

"Hmm… I close my eyes for one minute, and you're trying to steal what's mine."

Laughing, Kat says, "One minute? Try hours, honey."

Dane stands and hovers over his wife. "You should have woken me." He cups the side of her face and kisses her cheek. "Have you had any sleep?"

"Some."

Feeling like a third wheel, I back out of the room.

Dane notices and kisses his wife again. "I'm going to walk Dirt out. I'll be right back."

He follows me out and moves further down the hall. Kade stands near us.

"Do we know how Tobias is?"

"The same," I reply.

"Who's with him now?" Dane asks.

"Destiny."

Kade crosses his arms across his chest. "Was she okay?"

"I think so… told me to get her a coffee."

Dane runs a hand through his hair. "Keep me informed, yeah?"

"Will do, Prez."

Dane nods at me and goes back to his wife.

Retracing my steps, I hit the button for the elevator.

Kade taps me on the shoulder. "Can you tell Destiny to come see me before she leaves?"

"Will do." The elevator opens, I step inside, and then hit the button for the ground floor.

Walking into the lobby, paparazzi surround the outside of the hospital. Pushing past them, I pull out a packet of cigarettes and keep going until I'm away from the crowd. Taking out a cigarette, I put it in my mouth and light it. The first drag of nicotine instantly calms my nerves.

A car pulls into a spot near me, and a woman gets out. She's got dark glasses on, blonde streaked hair, and the other side of forty. She sees me looking and scowls. Being the gentleman I am, I give her a chin lift and take another pull of my smoke. She slams her car door, puts her handbag on her shoulder, and hurries toward me.

Reaching out, she plucks the cigarette from my lips, throws it on the ground, and grinds her boot on it.

"Jesus, lady, take a pill."

She puts her shades on her head and says, "Those things will kill you, Dirt."

"Lore?"

"And what the fuck did you and your MC do to my son?"

"What?"

"Tobias, what the fuck happened to him?"

"You're Tobias' mother?"

Turning, she storms away from me, shaking her head and shouting, "You always were quick on the uptake."

Lore Mercer, the only woman I've ever loved, just stormed back into my life. She was always a whirlwind of destruction and mayhem. It has to be ten years since I've seen her, and judging by the way she greeted me, time has not softened her one little bit.

TO BE CONTINUED

IN

Savage Heart

If you liked this story,
you can continue with
other books by Kathleen Kelly.

The MacKenny Brothers Series
An MC/Band of Brothers Romance
Spark Book 1
Spark of Vengeance Book 2
Spark of Hope Book 3
Spark of Deception Book 4
Spark of Time Book 5
Spark of Redemption Book 6

Tackling Romance Series
A Sports Romance
Tackling Love Book 1
Tackling Life Book 2

Standalones
Wraith
Cardinal: The Affinity Chronicles Book One
Crude Possession: Crude Souls MC
Snake's Revenge: Gritty Devils MC

The Savage Angels MC Series

Motorcycle Club Romance

Savage Stalker Book 1

Savage Fire Book 2

Savage Town Book 3

Savage Lover Book 4

Savage Sacrifice Book 5

Savage Rebel (Novella) Book 6

Savage Lies Book 7

Savage Life Book 8

Savage Christmas (Novella) Book 9

Check these links for more books from
Author Kathleen Kelly

READER GROUP

Want access to fun, prizes and sneak peeks?
Join my Facebook Reader Group.
https://bit.ly/32X17pv

NEWSLETTER

Want to see what's next?
Sign up for my Newsletter.
https://www.subscribepage.com/kathleenkellyauthor

BOOKBUB

Connect with me on Bookbub.
https://www.bookbub.com/authors/kathleen-kelly

GOODREADS

Add my books to your TBR list
on my Goodreads profile.
http://bit.ly/1xsOGxk

AMAZON

Buy my books from my Amazon profile.
https://amzn.to/2JCUT6q

WEBSITE

https://kathleenkellyauthor.com/

TIKTOK

https://www.tiktok.com/@kathleenkellyauthor

TWITTER

https://twitter.com/kkellyauthor

INSTAGRAM

https://instagram.com/kathleenkellyauthor

EMAIL

kathleenkellyauthor@gmail.com

FACEBOOK

https://bit.ly/36jlaQV

ABOUT THE AUTHOR

Kathleen Kelly was born in Penrith, NSW, Australia. When she was four, her family moved to Brisbane, QLD, Australia. Although born in NSW, she considers herself a QUEENSLANDER!

She married her childhood sweetheart, and they live in Toowoomba.

Kathleen enjoys writing contemporary romance novels with a little bit of steam. She draws her inspiration from family, friends, and the people around her. She can often be found in cafes writing and observing the locals.

If you have any questions about her novels or would like to ask Kathleen a question, she can be contacted via e-mail:

kathleenkellyauthor@gmail.com

or she can be found on Facebook. She loves to be contacted by those who love her books.

www.ingramcontent.com/pod-product-compliance
Lightning Source LLC
Chambersburg PA
CBHW051332020726
47501CB00007B/2048

* 9 7 8 1 9 2 2 8 8 3 0 7 0 *